2

L

"I want us to reverse course. To go back to the way we were. Before everything happened."

"As great as the idea sounds, I don't know if we can," she said honestly. "We aren't the same starry-eyed people we once were, and no amount of magical fairy dust will change us back."

He tugged her arm until she didn't have a choice but to perch on the edge of his bed. "Maybe we aren't the young, naive kids we once were. Maybe the hopes and dreams we once had have died. But that doesn't mean we can't create new ones. Together."

Darn it, but his grip was comforting, and once again his voice was so sincere—so full of faith—that the wall she'd created in her heart to hold back her hurts and disappointments began to crumble. Quickly she struggled to shore up those widening cracks, before emotions overwhelmed her.

Jessica Matthews's interest in medicine began at a young age, and she nourished it with medical stories and hospital-based television programmes. After a stint as a teenage candy-striper, she pursued a career as a clinical laboratory scientist. When not writing or on duty, she fills her day with countless family and school-related activities. Jessica lives in the central United States, with her husband, daughter and son.

Recent titles by the same author:

EMERGENCY: PARENTS NEEDED
THE ROYAL DOCTOR'S BRIDE

SIX-WEEK MARRIAGE MIRACLE

BY
JESSICA MATTHEWS

First published in Great Britain 2011
Harlequin Mills & Boon Limited,
Eton House, 18-24 Paradise Road, Richmond, Surrey TW9 1SR

© Jessica Matthews 2011

ISBN: 978 0 263 21882 4

Harlequin Mills & Boon policy is to use papers that are natural, renewable and recyclable products and made from wood grown in sustainable forests. The logging and manufacturing process conform to the legal environmental regulations of the country of origin.

Printed and bound in Great Britain
by CPI Antony Rowe, Chippenham, Wiltshire

SIX-WEEK MARRIAGE MIRACLE

To Judi Fennell for her Spanish language expertise.
Any errors are my own.

To adoptive and foster parents across the world.
Your generous spirit is truly an inspiration to all of us.

CHAPTER ONE

"ANOTHER ambulance is coming."

Leah Montgomery didn't spare her nursing colleague a glance as she stripped the used hospital sheets from the bed. "Tell me something I don't already know," she said wryly. "The moon was full when we came to work this morning."

Although it wasn't a scientific fact, hospital staff the world over recognized and accepted that full-moon shifts were the proverbial shifts from hell. So far, this was shaping up to be one of them. Everything from car wrecks, heart attacks, lawn mower accidents, and simple sore throats had flooded the Spring Valley ER on this hot August day.

While many of her staff bemoaned the extra workload, she didn't mind the increased pace at all. Being busy kept her mind off things she didn't want to think about—things like her husband's plane crashing in the Mexican jungle a month ago today. Or the report stating that there were no survivors, which meant Gabe was dead.

Dead!

After four painfully long weeks, it still seemed surreal, as if she might wake up some morning and discover she'd simply had a horrible nightmare. To her disappointment, each day was like the one before—the facts hadn't changed overnight. Neither did they change when she worked until she was too exhausted to reflect on the losses in her life.

If her boss would allow it, she'd cover more shifts than her PRN status allowed in order to keep her demons at bay. She was willing to do *anything* to stay busy until time took away the anguish over her last conversation with Gabe—the one where she'd asked to make their separation permanent with a divorce.

Some might call her crazy, others might say she was being silly and sentimental, but the truth was, she was mourning for Gabe on so many levels. Grieving that his vibrant life had been cut short at age thirty-eight; grieving that their marriage had reached an impasse; grieving for the loss of their dreams and missed opportunities. Was it any wonder she needed the fast pace of the hospital, the steady stream of new patients and drama as a life raft she could climb aboard?

"I hear Maternity is swamped," Jane rattled on, blithely unaware of Leah's inattention. "They're so packed with new moms, they're overflowing into the med-surg unit." She unfolded a fresh sheet and began tucking the corners under the mattress.

Leah pictured a nursery filled with bassinets of sleeping babies wearing pink or blue stocking hats, the hallway crowded with beaming fathers and proud grandparents while new mothers, some having already forgotten the pain of childbirth, looked on benevolently. She didn't begrudge the new families their happiness, but a familiar pang of disappointment shot through her chest.

At one time, she'd imagined herself in similar circumstances, with her parents waiting for their first peek at her child while Gabe passed out the bubblegum cigars and strutted as only a new father could. She'd fallen pregnant almost immediately after they'd decided it was time to start their family, making that dream seem like a sure thing and easily within her grasp. In her mind, and Gabe's, the future couldn't have been brighter.

Life, however, had rewritten her beautifully scripted scene.

Instead of joining the ranks of other new mothers, she'd become one of a small percentage of women who became a gynecological emergency. Shortly after entering her last trimester of an unremarkable pregnancy, her placenta had separated without warning. She'd lost the baby as well as her hopes for future children when profuse and unstoppable bleeding had necessitated a hysterectomy. Afterwards, she'd been whisked away to the surgical floor where babies weren't seen or heard.

Her parents had been there for her, of course, but pity, not pride, had shown on their faces. As for Gabe…he'd been on one of his occasional trips for the Montgomery family's medical foundation. He'd come as soon as her parents had called him, but time zones and flight schedules had prevented his return until the day she was ready to be released.

"I just love to stop and peek at the newborns," Jane gushed. "They have such cute little wrinkled faces." Suddenly, she stopped short. "Oh, Leah. Here I am, babbling on so insensitively about babies after everything you've been through. First a miscarriage, then the adoption fiasco—"

Leah cut off her friend's reminder of their failed foray into the world of adoption. After her surgery, still hazy from the grief of her loss, Gabe had convinced her to think about adoption and then so many things had fallen into place with amazing speed—Gabe's lawyer had known a young woman who'd wanted to relinquish her baby. They'd hurriedly filled out the necessary paperwork and completed the required governmental home studies and background checks. The entire time the birth mother had been adamant about her choice— she was making the right decision for both her and her unborn child. Yet when the hour arrived for Leah and Gabe to pick up the baby from the hospital, the young woman had changed her mind and Leah had once again driven home empty-handed.

Leah couldn't fault the girl for her change of heart—it had to be difficult to relinquish one's child, especially after seeing that tiny person for the first time—but understanding didn't take away her gut-wrenching disappointment.

"It's okay," she lied. "I don't fall apart just because someone talks about babies or mentions how cute they are."

Admittedly, they were, but seeing those adorable little faces was tough, which was why she never, *ever*, entered the secured area to stare at them through the plate-glass window. Why add insult to injury? she'd rationalized.

"I know, but—"

"It's okay," Leah repeated, as much for her own benefit as Jane's. "Honestly."

Jane nodded, but the worried wrinkle between her eyes suggested her good-mood bubble had burst. Determined to regain their easy footing, Leah thought it best to gently steer the conversation in another direction, for both their sakes.

"OB isn't the only busy department in this place," she commented as she tucked a fitted sheet around a corner of the mattress. "Our daily patient census is above average across the entire hospital and we both know our ED visit numbers are up, too. The extra business should make the bean counters happy."

"Maybe this year we'll get a Christmas bonus for a job well done," Jane responded hopefully.

Word from the last supervisors' meeting was that the possibility was remote, but Leah wasn't going to rain on Jane's picnic. "Maybe, but, bonus or not, more patients means more nursing staff are necessary, which means I work more often."

Jane paused from working on her own two bed corners. "Look, hon," she said kindly. "I know you're probably feeling guilty because you'd never resolved your differences with Gabe, but killing yourself now that he's gone, working sixty-plus hours a week, isn't the way to cope."

"I'm not killing myself," Leah protested mildly, pointedly ignoring Jane's opinion about her reasons for the pace she'd set for herself. "I'm merely keeping busy. Just like I have for the past year."

"Keeping busy is one thing. Doubling your hours is another."

"Okay, so I am working a few more hours," Leah conceded reluctantly, "but I was off duty yesterday and I spent the day puttering around the house. And then I treated myself to dinner and a movie."

"Dinner *and* a movie?" Jane's eyes brimmed with curiosity. "Did you *finally* put Jeff out of his misery and go on a *date*?"

About six months ago, Dr. Jeff Warren, one of Spring Valley's ED physicians, had invited her to a concert, then a community theater play. Both times she'd declined, not because she didn't enjoy his company or didn't want to attend those particular events. No, she'd gently refused his invitation because in spite of being separated from her husband of ten years, going out with another man while she was still officially married made her feel as if she was cheating.

Which was why she'd wanted Gabe's signature on those divorce papers. It was past time to stop expecting a miracle and start thinking about the future—*her* future—instead of the past. As it had turned out, she didn't need his signature after all.

Leah shot her friend a spare-me look. "Are you kidding?" she asked. "I haven't even buried Gabe and you're asking if I'm seeing Jeff?"

"Buried or not, you've been separated for over a year," Jane reminded her. "It's time to move on."

"I will," Leah promised. "But I can't until I've dotted all my 'i's and crossed all the 't's."

Jane rolled her eyes. "What's left to dot and cross? From what you've said, his body may never come home."

How well she knew that. The Mexican authorities had reported the discovery of the airplane's charred remains in a ravine. They lacked the resources to recover the bodies and in their bureaucratic minds the burned-out shell of the aircraft made it pointless to do so. Undaunted, and after greasing palms for several weeks, Gabe's second-in-command Sheldon Redfern had received permission to send in a private recovery team. As of yesterday, they hadn't reported any more encouraging news than what the authorities had already shared.

Their success, however, wasn't the reason she was dragging her feet...

"The annual foundation fund-raiser is coming up in a few months," she pointed out. "It seems tacky to plan a tribute to my deceased husband while I'm dating someone else." Their relationship may have been rocky the last two years and she might be finally ready to look for male companionship and find romance again, but in honor of the good times and the love they'd once shared, she owed it to Gabe to wait.

"Did you tell that to Jeff?"

She nodded, remembering their conversation. He'd been so understanding, which not only came as a relief but also endeared him to her all the more. "He's agreed to give me time," she said, deciding not to mention that she'd set their first official date for the Saturday night after the fundraiser. If Jane knew that, she'd be bouncing off the walls with excitement and Leah didn't want to see her sly smiles and winks in the meantime.

Jane stared at her thoughtfully. "Personally, I think you're worried too much about what other people think, but another month or two won't make much difference. Just be sure your decision to stay out of the dating game is based on the right reasons."

"What other reason could I have?"

Jane shrugged. "Oh, I don't know. Maybe that you still love Gabe and are waiting for the ultimate proof that he won't be coming back."

"Don't be ridiculous." She avoided her friend's gaze because she didn't want Jane to recognize what she herself refused to dwell on or admit. "If I loved him, why would I have moved out?"

"You tell me. I just don't want you to be stuck on hold for the rest of your life."

"I'm not," Leah insisted. "I'm merely being cautious. There's no sense rushing into something I might come to regret." She grabbed a fresh cotton blanket and shook it out of its folds with a decisive snap, effectively signaling an end to their conversation. "Do you know what's coming in next?"

Jane shook her head. "All I heard was that they were bringing in three from the airport."

"The airport?" She considered for a moment. "Bigwigs, no doubt."

"What makes you say that?"

"It's probably food related and the only folks who get food on a plane are seated in first class. And who usually can afford to sit in first class?"

"Ah." Jane's eyes gleamed. "Bigwigs."

"Exactly."

"You're stereotyping, you know. Regular people buy first-class tickets, too."

Leah flashed her a wide smile. "Okay, so I'm generalizing but, mark my words, it won't be three average Joes who roll into our ambulance bay. They'll be fellows wearing suits and ties, carrying briefcases and BlackBerrys, and wanting a magic pill to fix whatever ails them. Oh, and can we hurry because they're already late for a meeting."

Jane laughed, probably because Leah's scenario had actually taken place often enough to become a legend in the ER. "We'll find out if you're right in about three minutes. Marge wants us to be on the dock, ready to go."

As the emergency department's nurse manager, Marge Pennington was a person who believed in keeping busy every minute, so it seemed odd she would ask them to waste time waiting. Her request only seemed to substantiate Leah's prediction of several Very Important People arriving on this transport.

"Far be it from me to argue," she said, although it bothered her to think Marge was willing to discard her normal habits in order to impress people with money. Having married into a family with the Midas touch, Leah had always been leery of people who didn't treat her as they would anyone else.

"According to her, the person radioing in specifically asked for you."

Leah's eyes widened. "Me? Why me?"

Jane shrugged. "Maybe it's someone you know from Gabe's trust organization."

Leah mentally ran through her list of regularly gener- ous contributors to the Montgomery Medical Charitable Foundation. As chairwoman of the annual fund-raising ball, which would take place in six weeks, she was acquainted with nearly all of the supporters, but none knew she worked in the Spring Valley Hospital Emergency Department.

"Impossible," she said.

Jane shrugged. "Who knows? In any case, I'm only fol- lowing Marge's orders and if you know what's good for you, you will, too."

Marge wasn't the easiest charge nurse to work for, but she was a model of efficiency and a brilliant nurse. No one, not even the hospital's CEO, crossed her when she was in battle mode.

Leah gave the bed a final pat, pleased with their results. "Okay, then. Let's go. I can use a few minutes of fresh air while we're waiting." She grinned. "Just think, we might even get to sit and rest our weary feet."

Outside, Leah did exactly as she'd hoped to. Ignoring Jane and the two extra staff who'd joined them with wheelchairs and an extra stretcher, she sat on the concrete loading dock and dangled her legs over the edge as she breathed in the fresh air and soaked up the heat.

If only the summer sun would chase away the coldness inside her—the same coldness that had settled into every cell, the same coldness that had taken hold ever since she'd realized Gabe's plane had gone down with her request for a divorce ringing in his ears.

She'd agonized for weeks over taking their separation to its logical conclusion before she'd contacted a lawyer, but they'd lived apart for nearly a year. After the adoption had fallen through, they'd simply shut down. It was understand- able, she supposed. They'd been obsessed with the baby when she'd been pregnant, and then they'd focused exclusively on adopting a child. Their marriage had been so driven toward that end goal that their sudden failure had simply sidelined their relationship.

Consequently they'd drifted apart until the only solution had been to ask for a change of scenery. She'd wanted time and space to redefine what she wanted out of life and, more importantly, she wanted Gabe to have the same.

A year later, she'd finally faced the facts. Remaining in their legal limbo wasn't doing either of them any favors. They both needed the freedom to pursue their dreams—she wanted companionship and Gabe wanted a family. Although she hated the idea of Gabe finding a woman who could give him what she couldn't, it had seemed silly, selfish and almost spiteful to keep him from his heart's desire. With the stroke of a judge's pen, they would end their estranged state and could move on with their lives. To start over, as it were.

In the end, her altruistic decision had been wasted. Fate had stepped in and had the last laugh at their expense before he could sign the papers dissolving their marriage. Before he'd created the family he'd always wanted.

Since then, she'd told herself on a daily basis to stop beating herself over everything from procrastinating to her bad timing. After all, divorced or widowed, she was still alone.

Alone or not, though, it pained her to imagine what final thoughts had run through Gabe's head. No doubt his last one of her had involved the unpleasant scene when she'd asked for a divorce. Some would say she was being too hard on herself. Others would say she was worrying over nothing. After all, if she wanted to completely sever their matrimonial ties, why did she care what his last thoughts of her had been?

In one corner of her heart, she'd wanted Gabe to realize their marriage needed as much attention as he gave his family's charitable foundation, but if he'd entertained any regrets during his final moments, she'd never know. Chances were, she repeated to herself for the millionth time, he hadn't thought of her at all…

Jane straightened, her gaze riveted in the distance. "Looks

like they're about two blocks away." She glanced at her watch. "Right on time, too."

Leah slowly got to her feet then brushed the seat of her scrub pants. "I wish we knew what we were getting," she fretted.

"We'll find out soon enough."

A black Lexus squealed to an abrupt stop in the aisle of the parking lot. Apparently the driver didn't care about the traffic snarl he'd created.

"Security is going to eat him alive," Leah commented.

"Maybe you should tell him."

The ambulance pulled in and began backing up to the dock, its warning beeps intermingling with the other city noises. "He'll have to take his chances," Leah said. "We have things to do and people to see."

As the ambulance inched backwards, Leah heard someone call her name. A familiar figure, Sheldon Redfern had jumped out of the Lexus and was running toward her.

"Leah," he panted. "Wait!"

"Sheldon, what are you doing here?" she asked, amazed to see him.

"I have to tell you—"

The ambulance braked. "Save it for later," she ordered. "I'm busy right now."

"This can't wait."

He grabbed her arm at the same time she saw Jane twisting the handle to open the back door. "Sheldon," she protested. "I have work to do."

"Leah," he urged. "It's about Gabe and the search team we sent."

Instinctively, her heart sank. Sheldon's eagerness to contact her only meant one thing.

"They finally located his remains," she said dully, feeling her chest tighten and a painful knot clog her throat as her eyes dimmed with sudden tears. For all the problems they'd had, she hadn't wanted anything so drastic and so *final* to happen to him. Yes, a divorce was like a death—the death of a marriage—but part of her consolation had been that they each would carry on and eventually find the happiness they couldn't find with each other.

Unfortunately, Sheldon's announcement had irrevocably destroyed that thin hope. Why had he felt compelled to deliver the news now, *at this very moment*, with patients breathing down her neck, when she wasn't mentally prepared to deal with the finality of the situation?

"No," Sheldon corrected in her ear.

"No?" She stared at him in surprise.

"What he's trying to say unsuccessfully is that they found *us*." Sheldon's voice suddenly sounded closer...and deeper... and more like...Gabe's.

And it was coming from inside the ambulance.

She focused in that direction, ignoring the paramedic to glance at the human cargo—two men and a woman. They looked tired and dirty in clothing that was tattered and torn, but broad smiles shone on their faces. An uncanny sense of familiarity struck her.

In spite of their gaunt and disreputable appearance, she *knew* all three. Yet her brain couldn't reconcile what she was seeing with what she'd been told.

She homed in on the man who'd spoken. He was just as dirty as the other two and equally as disheveled. His right pants leg had been cut open at some point but in spite of being tied closed with strips of gauze, she glimpsed a white bandage circling his shin. A splint encased his left forearm and another bandage was visible above the open neck of his torn shirt. But there was no denying that this man was Gabe.

"I tried calling you all morning," Sheldon babbled in the background as the identities of Gabe's colleagues— Jack Kasold and Theresa Hernandez—registered before they stepped onto the concrete. "You never answered my messages."

The pink scraps of paper tucked in her tunic pocket suddenly weighed like the proverbial ton of bricks. She'd ignored them when she'd seen who'd phoned because she'd assumed he simply wanted to hash out more details for the foundation's upcoming charity ball. Apparently, she'd been wrong.

"I was going to call you during my break," she said numbly as she looked past all the people to study her husband once again.

Tape bisected his forehead, his beard was scruffy, his hair shaggy, and lines of apparent pain bracketed his full mouth, but his midnight-black eyes were so familiar.

Could it be true? Really *true*? Her heart skipped a beat as she feared she might be hallucinating and hoped she was not.

"Gabe?" she finally asked, aware of how thin and reedy her voice sounded.

He stepped out of the ambulance, balancing himself on one crutch. His reassuring smile was one she'd seen before—the same one that belonged to the man she'd married when their future had been bright and it had seemed as if nothing could stop them from living their dreams.

"Hi, honey. I'm home."

CHAPTER TWO

UNCERTAIN of the reception he'd receive when he finally saw Leah again, Gabriel's tension had escalated with each mile closer to his destination. Considering how Sheldon hadn't been able to reach her all morning, Gabe had expected her to be surprised and shocked by his astonishing return and she didn't disappoint him.

"Gabe?" she whispered in that soft voice he remembered so vividly. "Is it really *you*?"

He met her gaze and offered a rueful smile. "A little the worse for wear but, yes, it is."

"Oh, my." She covered her mouth with both hands. Suddenly, she turned pale and a dazed look came to her eyes.

She was going to faint. Cursing because he wasn't in a position to catch her himself, he roared, "Sheldon!"

Fortunately, his second-in-command was beside her and grabbed her arm. At the same time the paramedic did the same. For an instant she sagged, then straightened and shrugged off the two men's hold.

"I'm okay," she insisted, losing a bit of her deer-caught-in-the-headlights look.

"Are you sure?" The paramedic didn't sound convinced as he eyed her closely.

"I'm fine. Really."

Of course she was, Gabe thought wryly. Leah thrived on her ability to handle anything and everything by herself, without help from anyone. In fact, at times he'd felt rather superfluous in their marriage, but he intended to change all that.

"Truly," she insisted, tentatively reaching toward him.

Eager to touch her and prove just how wrong the reports of his death had been, as well as to reassure himself that he was truly home, Gabe grabbed her hand.

Her skin was soft and warm and soothingly familiar. Oh, how he'd missed her!

Before he could say a word, before he could do anything but entwine his fingers with hers, she flung herself against him and buried her face in his shoulder.

His crutch clattered to the concrete and his ribs protested, but having her in his arms where she belonged was worth the pain. When his plane had landed and Leah hadn't been standing with Jack's and Theresa's elated families on the tarmac, he'd been so afraid...but this was the response he'd dreamed of and hoped for every night they'd been lost in the jungle.

The coldness of despair, the survivor's guilt, and the soul-racking regret that he'd labored under for weeks now began to diminish until he slowly felt warm from the inside out.

His wife's fresh, clean scent filled his nostrils and reminded him of how desperately he needed soap and water. If he'd been thinking properly, he might have asked Sheldon to detour to his corporate offices where he could have made use of the executive washroom, but he'd been too eager to see Leah to consider it. Quite frankly, though, with his stiff shoulder and the slow-healing gash on his leg, he wasn't sure he could manage the feat on his own, anyway.

He gripped her with his good arm, feeling her slight frame shake beneath his hand. As her tears soaked his shirt, his throat tightened and his eyes burned with more emotion than he could begin to describe.

"Oh, honey. Don't cry," he said hoarsely, relieved by her reception and grateful the paramedics and ER staff were giving them a few minutes before they whisked him away.

"I'm not," she sniffed, swiping at the moisture on her cheeks as she stared at him. "Oh, Gabe. I can't believe it."

As he gazed at her, one thought ran through his mind. She was beautiful—more beautiful than the picture he'd slipped out of his wallet and stuck in his shirt pocket shortly after they'd crashed. The photo was now dog-eared and a little dirty, but her image had given him the incentive to keep going when he'd sworn he couldn't hobble another step.

"I can't quite believe it, either," he said ruefully. As far as he was concerned, this was a dream come true. A bona fide miracle.

More importantly, it was a miracle he wasn't going to let slip through his fingers.

"What happened?" she asked.

"It's a long story." Rather than dwell on that fateful day and the events leading up to it, he drank in everything about her, from her acorn-colored hair and eyes that reminded him of the Grand Canyon's various shades of brown to her retroussé nose and sensual mouth. She'd lost weight, too, if his hands hadn't deceived him.

The paramedic stepped close to interrupt. "I don't mean to cut short your reunion, Dr. Montgomery, but let's get you inside before you fall."

Whether she suddenly realized how heavily he was leaning against her or the paramedic's statement had reminded her of his injuries, his prim and proper wife—and she still *was* his wife, even if they'd lived apart for the last twelve months—unwrapped herself from him and took his good arm. Although he missed her embrace, he was glad she hadn't completely turned him loose. Granted, she'd fallen back into nurse mode, but he wanted to believe she needed the contact as much as he did to reassure herself that he was, indeed, alive and well.

Maybe not "well", he corrected as he lowered himself into a hastily provided wheelchair, but his aches and pains now seemed inconsequential. For the past month he'd fought his fears of failure—fears that the feelings she'd once had for him were gone—but he took heart that she hadn't rejected him. In the nightmares that had often startled him awake, he'd dreamt she'd take one look at him and walk away. Thankfully, none of those painfully vivid dreams had come true.

They still had issues to resolve but he was cautiously optimistic about success. If he played his cards right—and he intended to because he'd had a month to plan a strategy—there wouldn't be any more talk of a divorce. Fate had given him a second chance to correct his mistakes and undo the past. He would not fail.

Leah wanted to ask a hundred questions, but Gabe's slumped shoulders as she walked beside his wheelchair told her how exhausted he was. In all the years she'd known him, she'd never seen him so drained, even during his residency when forty-eight-hour shifts had been the norm. There would be plenty of time to hear his story after his medical needs were addressed—starting with how he'd survived a supposedly fatal accident.

It wasn't until he'd gingerly moved from his wheelchair to the bed with her help and that of a paramedic that she realized the awkwardness of the situation. As a nurse she belonged in the room, but as his estranged wife she certainly didn't. Unfortunately, by the time she'd come to that conclusion, the other nurses had already disappeared into their respective patients' rooms, leaving her no choice but to continue. Asking for a reassignment now would only draw unwanted and unnecessary attention. As soon as word leaked of Gabe's return, speculation would run rampant anyway.

In spite of resigning herself to her temporary fate, her awkwardness grew exponentially as Jeff Warren took that moment to walk into the room. The normally implacable blond physician stopped abruptly in his tracks, as if he hadn't realized the identity of his patient until now. Immediately, he glanced back at Leah and she shrugged helplessly, realizing that this moment was as uncomfortable for him as it was for her. The only difference was Jeff seemed to recover more quickly from his surprise than she had.

"Gabe," he said, reaching out to shake his hand. "Welcome back."

"Thanks. It's great to be home."

"I'll do my best to get you there," Jeff promised. "Let's have a look at what you've done to yourself, shall we?"

Leah had planned to act as usual, giving Gabe the same objective care she'd give any other patient. However, that was easier said than done. The minute he shrugged off his tattered shirt, she saw the physical evidence of what he'd endured. His bones stood out in stark relief to the scabbed-over scrapes and large, brilliantly colored patches of purple, yellow and green that dotted his skin, while other areas were rubbed raw.

"Oh, Gabe," she breathed.

"It looks worse than it is," he assured her.

Objectively speaking, he was probably right, but through the eyes of someone who'd once carefully and lovingly mapped every inch of his six-foot body, she wasn't as certain. It became far too easy to imagine how he'd earned each scrape and each bruise and then marvel at how he'd endured the trauma and still returned home. His obvious weight loss made her wonder what he'd eaten, if anything, which was another facet of his ordeal she hadn't considered until now.

Part of her wanted to hug him again, to erase those physical hurts with a soft and gentle touch. The other part of her wanted to rail at him, ask if his injuries had been worth those extra duties he'd assumed and the additional trips he'd taken on behalf of his family's charitable organization.

More importantly, though, she wanted to lock herself in the restroom so she could cry because, however illogical it seemed, she somehow felt responsible—not for the crash itself, or even for this particularly fateful international jaunt, but for sending him into the ever-eager arms of the Montgomery Medical Foundation. Had she not rejected his comfort after their adoption had fallen through, he wouldn't have found his purpose in his work. With the schedule he'd set for himself, both before their separation and after, it was almost amazing that disaster hadn't struck before now.

Regardless of where she laid blame or how she took responsibility, what mattered most for now was the state of Gabe's health, not rehashing the mistakes or hurts of the past.

"Leah?"

Hearing her name, she pulled her thoughts together and met Jeff's questioning gaze. He was obviously reading more into her inattentiveness than she wanted.

"Maybe you should take a break," he suggested softly.

She was tempted to take his advice, but she'd never deserted a patient before and she wouldn't start now. She shook her head and squared her shoulders. "I'm fine. Really."

Jeff simply shrugged, then listened to Gabe's chest sounds as he spoke. "You still have some nasty injuries. What did you do? Hit every tree in the jungle?"

"It seemed like it," Gabe mentioned ruefully. "I picked up about half of my bruises and bumps during the crash. Splitting my leg open came later."

"What happened?"

"In regard to my leg or the crash itself?"

"Both."

Curious about the details surrounding his experience, Leah listened closely.

"Minutes before we crashed, there was a thump, then an engine sputtered, and Ramon yelled something about birds. The next thing I knew, we were going down." He paused. "When it was all over, I had a dislocated shoulder and a bad wrist. Jack relocated the bone and immobilized my arm with the supplies out of our first-aid kit. Then we went to find help."

Leah tried not to imagine the pain he must have endured while Jack had worked on his shoulder without any anesthetic. As an internist, Jack's basic orthopedic skills were no doubt rusty, but he would have had to proceed because the potential complications like a lack of blood supply and damaged nerves were too serious to ignore. As she surreptitiously studied Gabe's fingers, the pink skin color and lack of swelling were reassuring signs of his success.

"Needless to say, it took us a while to find another human being," he added wryly, "although, technically, a few locals found us when they stumbled across our path. We stayed in their village overnight but before they took us to the next town, the search team had tracked us there. And here we are."

"You're lucky they found you at all," Leah interjected. "We were told you were dead." Thank goodness Sheldon had persisted with cutting through the red tape to send in their own team. If they'd accepted the official verdict and let matters lie... the idea of Gabe and his colleagues still wandering through the jungle sent a chill down her spine.

"I'm not surprised the authorities assumed the worst," Gabe said, his voice pained. "We'd stopped inches away from a ravine and thought we were on safe ground. Not long afterwards, the ground gave way and the plane slid over the edge. On its way down, the fuel tanks blew."

Mentally picturing the scene, Leah shuddered as her grip tightened on the blood-pressure cuff she was still holding.

"You three are celebrities now," Jeff remarked. "Not many people walk away from an experience like that."

Gabe's face became stoic, his expression shuttered. "Two of my group didn't."

"Who?" she asked, hating it that not everyone associated with Montgomery Medical would have a happy ending.

"Will. Will Henderson, and Ramon."

Will was an information technology guru Gabe had hired about eighteen months ago to facilitate the internet connections between remote medical clinics and hospitals to specialists at centers like Spring Valley. Leah had met him a few times but had never had any dealings with him.

Ramon Diaz, however, was a man she knew quite well. As the first pilot Gabe had ever hired and the organization's most senior pilot, Ramon had usually taken charge of Gabe's flights. He'd also begun dating Theresa, one of the foundation's nurses, right before Leah and Gabe had split up, and had recently proposed to her. No doubt they'd both been thrilled to go on this trip together. How sad it had ended so horribly.

"Oh, Gabe," she breathed, knowing how the loss of two people who had been more friends than employees must weigh heavily on him. She dropped the cuff and clutched his hand in sympathy. "Did they…suffer?"

"Will didn't. He died in the crash. Ramon…died later."

Gabe's tight-lipped expression suggested there was a lot more to his story, but she didn't press for details. "I'm sorry, both for you and the company. Theresa must be devastated."

"She's having a tough time," Gabe agreed.

Making a mental note to visit with Theresa as soon as she was able, Leah watched as Jeff unwrapped the bandage around Gabe's leg. The gash was red and swollen, but didn't look nearly as bad as Leah had anticipated.

"I've seen worse," the doctor remarked, apparently agreeing with her opinion. "How long ago did this happen?"

"About ten days. I slid down a hill and bumped into a few rocks along the way. One of them sliced my skin."

"Then it definitely isn't healing as fast as I'd like."

"We cleaned it as best we could but, as you can see, our topical ointment couldn't quite do the job." Gabe winced as his colleague probed the area and his grip on her hand tightened. "Sutures might have helped, but those weren't available, either."

Leah wasn't fooled by his innocent tone or his condensed version of events. He could probably talk for hours about their struggle for the things she took for granted—food, water, protection from the elements and safety from predators. And he'd definitely had a difficult time because his clothing appeared as if he'd walked through a shredder.

As for his injuries, he'd made them sound as if they were nothing more than minor inconveniences when they were visible proof of his harrowing ordeal. Cracked ribs and a dislocated shoulder were painful under ideal conditions and to "slide down a hill and bump into a few rocks" before they'd healed would have been agony. If the truth were known, it wouldn't surprise her to learn that his so-called "hill" could probably compete with Pikes Peak and his "few rocks" had probably been boulders.

She wanted to throttle him for acting as if his stint in the jungle had been as easy and effortless as a Sunday stroll through the city park. Making a big deal out of bumps and bruises, gashes and cracked bones went against his macho grain, even if he was speaking to a physician who recognized what it took to create this degree of damage. There were two females in the room, too, and it wouldn't do to appear weak in front of them. In essence, it was a guy thing—part of that caveman, show-the-woman-who's-strongest mentality.

It was also a Gabe thing. He'd always tried his best to insulate her from the harsh realities of life instead of treating her as a partner in the challenges they faced—and they'd had a number of personal difficulties and tragedies to contend with. Obviously, he still pictured her as being too weak to face the truth. While some women might appreciate being treated like a Fabergé egg, she wasn't one of them. After ten years of marriage, Gabe should have learned that, but he hadn't.

As soon as she recognized the familiar resentment building inside her, she wondered why her former frustrations were rearing their heads again. She should be elated Gabe was home safe and more or less sound and not dredging up old complaints. Her only excuse was that she could finally give herself permission to be angry about his decision to take this flight in the first place.

Yet, however one might psychoanalyze her reaction, Gabe's return didn't wipe their slate of problems clean. They still had to be addressed in some manner and the easiest and most expedient method was to get his signature on those divorce documents, wherever they currently were.

Realizing her fingers were still entwined with his, she pulled her hand free.

Jeff's gaze was speculative as he glanced at her. He'd clearly noticed how her touch had lingered longer than was actually necessary, but he didn't comment. Instead, he finished his exam and tucked his stethoscope back into his pocket with deliberate movements.

"All things considered," he said, "you're not in too bad a shape." He paused ever so slightly as his gaze slid sideways to Leah and then back to Gabe. "You're a lucky fellow in more ways than one."

"You don't have to remind me," Gabe answered fervently.

A meaningful note in his tone made Leah question if the two men were discussing Gabe's health or if this was some sort of private male discussion, but before she could wade into the conversation, Jeff fell back into his professional mode.

"You've probably diagnosed yourself, but I want X-rays to check your ribs and your arm as well as basic bloodwork and cultures. To be honest, I'm not happy with the way your leg is healing, so prepare yourself for a few rounds of IV antibiotics." He glanced at Leah. "I want those started immediately."

Considering the state of Gabe's leg, Jeff's treatment plan was not only sound, it was necessary to stop the infection from turning septic. Without a word, she began pulling the appropriate IV supplies from the cabinet.

Gabe sighed audibly, as if he also knew the IV was necessary but wasn't particularly happy about it. "I'd expected as much."

"I'm glad we agree. After I see the films and lab results, we'll talk again."

"Any chance I can shower in the doctors' lounge before you run me through the testing mill?" Gabe's expression was hopeful. He might be the full-time CEO of the Montgomery Medical Foundation but he was also a member of the surgical staff at Spring Valley Memorial and, as such, he filled in a few nights a month and the occasional weekend when the regular surgeons took time off.

"Of course," Jeff agreed, "but if we delay your tests, we also delay your treatment. So let's do the cultures, blood samples and X-rays first, then by the time you finish your shower, we'll have answers and can decide what comes next."

Knowing how Gabe hated to compromise, Leah expected him to argue, but to her surprise, he didn't. "Okay. If it means I'll get out of here sooner, we'll do it your way."

Jeff grinned. "I'm glad to hear it. While you're stuck in Radiology, I'll see about arranging for first-class bathroom accommodations." He turned to Leah. "He's all yours for now."

It was a throw-away statement, a figure of speech, but she wondered if his qualifier referred to tending Gabe's injuries or if it had more personal overtones. Because it was far easier to fall back on the comforting routine of following a doctor's orders, she did so, determined to leave the soul-searching for later when her mind had stopped reeling.

Thank goodness experience allowed her to perform her tasks without thinking as she still considered Gabe's return as nothing short of miraculous. Thankfully, and perhaps Jeff had alerted Marge to the situation, Jane came in to help.

"Stay," Gabe said when Leah tried to escape, and so she did, but by the time he'd finished the lab draws and X-rays, his face was white and pinched with pain. Clearly, he was in desperate need of rest.

"I think the shower should wait," she began.

His jaw squared. "No way."

"Not even until you've napped a few hours?"

"Not even then."

Seeing how unsteady he was on his feet, she offered, "How about a sponge bath instead?"

His eyes lit with an unholy gleam before it faded. "As intriguing as that sounds, I want a shower that lasts until I empty the hot water tanks. I *need* a shower because I'm tired of smelling myself."

"You smell fresher than some patients who've walked through our doors," she replied.

"Too bad. I know what I want and I want water. Gallons and gallons of it."

"But you can hardly—"

His gaze was determined. "Trust me. I can and *will* do whatever I have to."

She wanted him to be reasonable and take her advice, but if he'd found the fortitude to survive the jungle, he'd find the energy reserves to shower. However, as both his nurse and his wife, she'd watch to ensure he didn't over-extend himself.

"You always were stubborn," she remarked.

He nodded. "I'll take that as a compliment."

"Well, hang tight while I see what I can arrange."

After a short consultation in the hallway where she couldn't speak privately to Jeff because Jane was part of their group, Leah wheeled Gabe to the nearby med-surg wing and into a patient room. She expected him to protest at the obvious implication, but he was too intent on his prize and didn't.

While he brushed his teeth with the spare toiletry kit she'd commandeered from their supply cabinet, she located towels and soap so he could finally indulge in his much-wanted and much-needed shower in the wheelchair-accessible bathroom.

After removing his splint—the X-ray had shown the bones in his arm and shoulder weren't broken—she covered his IV site with plastic so it wouldn't get wet.

"I'll be out here if you need me," she told him. "Be careful with your leg and when you're finished, I'll dress it."

While he hobbled into the shower, she turned down his bed and double-checked the medications that Jane had delivered. When she had everything in place except for her patient, she returned to the bathroom and stood in the doorway.

"How are you doing in there?" She raised her voice over the rushing water, noting he'd had at least a seven-minute shower.

"Fine." A groan came from behind the curtain.

That didn't sound good. Instantly worried, she straightened, ready to invade his privacy. "Are you okay?"

"Yeah. God, this feels so good."

The awe in his voice reminded her of other times when

he'd said the same, under more intimate circumstances. She quickly stuffed those thoughts inside her mental box labeled "to be opened at a later date". "I'm sure it does, but Jeff wants those antibiotics started ASAP."

"Just a few more minutes."

"The shower will still be here, waiting for you, tomorrow," she coaxed.

"I know, but five more minutes. Please."

It seemed cruel to deny him this simple pleasure when those extra minutes probably wouldn't affect his treatment outcome. "Okay, but I'm timing you."

"You're the boss."

If that were only true.

"I'd get done faster if you scrubbed my back for me," he added.

He sounded so hopeful and so like the old Gabe—the Gabe before their lives had drifted apart—that she flashed back to those happier times when they *had* shared a shower. The memory of the subsequent lovemaking burst into her head, but it was more than simple recall. She replayed how it had *felt*—from the sensation of his rough skin against hers, the tickle of his breath and his lips on sensitive areas, his clean, sandalwood scent teasing her nose.

His suggestion was so very tempting...especially when she reflected on their stolen moments during the early days of their relationship. In his position as a surgical resident and hers as a newly minted ED nurse, as long as a deadbolt guarded their privacy, they'd been happy.

Unfortunately, they didn't have a locked door and Gabe had become a celebrity, which meant privacy was impossible. Although those details didn't present an insurmountable problem, making love at this point implied that their personal life was fine and dandy.

And it wasn't.

"Not a good idea," she pointed out.

"Why not?"

"You mean, other than that you're barely able to stand?"

"Yeah."

"This place will be like Grand Central Station before long," she reminded him. "Everyone wants to drop by and give you a personal welcome."

"They can wait. Besides, people will understand if we have a quiet, intimate reunion. They're probably expecting it, which means no one will interrupt us unless there's a fire."

The sad fact was he was probably right. Most people knew they were separated, but no one, other than Jane, knew the D-word had been floated between them. Everyone loved a happy ending, which meant everyone would speculate—if not hope—that Gabe's return would be the turning point in their relationship. Perhaps under other circumstances, it would have been, but their differences were more deep-seated than a conversation or a few promises could fix.

"They can expect all they want, but it isn't going to happen."

His sigh was audible. "I suppose not, but I really would like you to wash my back. I can't reach."

Instantly, she felt ashamed for not realizing how his bruised ribs and stiff shoulder made his request completely valid. Irritated at herself for jumping to the wrong conclusion, she shoved the curtain aside to see her dripping husband struggling to touch those hard-to-reach places.

"Turn around," she ordered, determined to handle her task with clinical detachment. Yet, as she ignored the spray of water on her scrub suit to run a soapy washcloth down his spine and over the lean muscles of his back before moving around to his front, her concern over what he'd endured grew. This wasn't the body of the man she'd last seen a month ago. Oh, the birthmark in the small of his back was the same, as was the general shape of his torso, but while he'd once reminded her of a lean mountain lion with rock-hard muscles and sinew, now he resembled a starving wolf.

"If you keep that up," he said dryly, "our private reunion will be extremely one-sided."

Realizing she'd come dangerously close to an area of his body where she hadn't intended to go, she froze.

"Although," he added softly, "there's always later."

The promise in his voice sent an unexpected tingle through her body but, then, a mere glance, a simple touch, or a softly spoken word from Gabe had always carried enough power to melt her into a puddle. What truly surprised her was how she could respond so easily in spite of the issues that had driven them apart. Was she so starved for attention and affection that when he showered her with both, she would greedily accept it?

Disliking what her response suggested, she dropped the washcloth over the handrail. "Rinse off. I'll be waiting." Suddenly realizing what she'd said, she clarified. "Outside. I'll be waiting *outside.*"

As he laughed, she flung the curtain closed and counted to twenty so Gabe could finish and she could recover her composure.

"Time's up," she called.

He didn't respond.

"Gabe?" she repeated. "Your time is up."

Still no answer.

"Gabe?" Although she hadn't heard a thump or other worrisome noise, his silence raised her concern. She flung back the curtain once again to find him leaning against the tiled wall, his eyes closed, his dark hair dripping.

"I knew it," she scolded as she cranked the taps until the water stopped. "You've stayed in here too long. You're about to fall on your face."

"Maybe, but being clean would be worth it."

CHAPTER THREE

GABE hated feeling weak. For a man whose body had never failed him before, it was a humbling experience to be at less than peak condition. However, if his injuries convinced Leah to give him another chance, he wouldn't complain too loudly.

Although, in spite of his aches and pains, he'd been relieved to discover one part of his body still worked quite well. If he hadn't stopped her from toweling him off like a child, he would have needed a second shower—an ice-cold one.

"I don't suppose I can wear a scrub suit instead of that," he said, eyeing the hospital gown she held out.

"We'd never be able to take care of your leg if you were wearing trousers."

"I could wear a pair of athletic shorts."

"You could," she agreed, "but a pair isn't available at the moment. You're stuck with this for now."

"You could cut off the legs and turn the pants into shorts," he coaxed.

"If you were going to stay a few days, I would, but I suspect you're not, so I won't. Now, stop arguing." She tied the string at the back of his neck then guided him to the nearby bed.

He sank gratefully onto the mattress before he rubbed his face. "Did you bring a razor?"

"Not this trip. Count your blessings for the toothbrush I found. Would you like to sit or lie down?"

"Sit."

She immediately adjusted the bed to accommodate his wishes then pulled the sheet over his good leg, leaving his injured extremity uncovered while she fluffed his pillows. "We'll tackle the beard later. You've done enough for the moment."

He hated to admit she was right, but although his spirit was willing, his flesh was weak. He'd been functioning on adrenalin for too long. Now that he'd enjoyed a hot shower, although a much shorter one than he would have liked, he'd crash soon. With any luck, after a rejuvenating nap, his IV would have run its course and he could convince Leah to drive him home, where he'd deal with the proverbial elephant in the room.

"Maybe," he conceded, fighting to keep his eyes open. "But the beard has to go. It itches."

"We'll get to it," she promised, "but first things first." She reattached his IV tubing to the port just above his wrist before he recognized his surroundings.

Suspicion flared. Patients weren't shown to a regular room if they were leaving the hospital in a few hours. "What am I doing here?"

"Jeff ordered IV fluids and antibiotics. Remember?"

"I know that," he snapped. "Why am I *here*, instead of back in Emergency?"

Jeff strolled in at that moment, carrying films and a fistful of paper. "You're here, Gabe, because I'm admitting you for observation."

"I don't need observing. I'm fi—"

Jeff held up his hands. "Yes, you're fine," he said in a placating tone, "but you could be better and that's what we're going to do—make you better. I showed your X-rays to Smithson in Orthopedics and he agrees with me. You suffered a severe sprain to your wrist when you dislocated your shoulder. According to him, your shoulder is okay but he recommends a wrist brace for a few weeks." He peered over his reading glass with a warning glare, "However, he still wants you to take things easy, so don't lift anything heavier than a pen for a while."

Gabe took the films to see for himself. "Fair enough."

"As for your ribs," Jeff continued, "they'll get better on their own, provided you slow down and rest. But you already know that."

Jeff's advice fell in line with Gabe's plans, as he'd hoped it would.

"My main concern," Jeff continued, "is infection and I want to hit those bugs hard." He glanced at the IV pole. "I see your antibiotics are running."

"Thanks to my ever-efficient nurses," Gabe quipped.

"I'm glad you agree because you're going to be at their tender mercy for a few days."

His jaw squared as he shook his head. "No can do. I'm going home."

Jeff shook his head. "Not a good idea, buddy."

"Good idea or not, I'm sleeping in my own bed tonight. I can either do it with your permission or I'll check myself out AMA." Gabe hated to play the against-medical-advice card against a colleague, but he was *home*, dammit, and he wasn't going to postpone his heart-to-heart with Leah another day. He had too much to say and he couldn't say any of it here where walls were paper-thin and interruptions were commonplace.

"I can't give you my blessing to leave in a few hours." Jeff emphasized his statement with a brisk shake of his head. "I honestly can't."

"Are you keeping Theresa and Jack?" Gabe demanded.

"No, but, unlike a certain person, they only need good food and rest to recover from their experience," Jeff said wryly, "not high-powered antibiotics."

"If the IV is stopping you, I can handle it. Or Leah can do the honors. Just give her the supplies and we'll take it from there." Gabe heard her muffled gasp, but ignored it to fix his gaze on his doctor.

Jeff pursed his mouth as his eyes darted between Leah

and Gabe. "She could," he finally agreed, "but you know the dangers of septicemia as well as I do. You belong here where we can monitor you." He held up his hands to forestall his objections. "At least until the lab gives me preliminary culture results."

"Sorry. I'll stay a few hours to finish this IV, but I'm going home tonight."

After muttering something about physicians being terrible patients, Jeff turned to Leah. "Talk some sense into him, will you?"

She shrugged. "Sorry, but you're on your own. If he won't listen to you, he certainly won't listen to me."

Her matter-of-fact tone surprised Gabe. Did she really believe that he didn't value her opinion? And yet, in hindsight, he could understand how she might feel that way. After they'd lost their son and their dreams of having a child of their own, he'd wanted to do *something* to make things right again. When the opportunity to adopt a baby had literally fallen into his lap, he'd gone full-steam ahead over her halfhearted objections when he should have allowed Leah—and himself—more time to deal with their first loss. In the end, they'd had *two* losses to cope with and clearly hadn't done well with either.

Regardless, he'd had weeks to reflect on their relationship and if he wanted to prove to her that he was giving his marriage and her opinions top priority, then this was his opportunity.

"I'm listening now," he pointed out, avoiding references to the past in order to avoid a potential argument. "What do *you* suggest I do?"

"Follow your doctor's instructions," she said bluntly. "Jeff isn't being unreasonable."

No, Jeff wasn't, but Gabe hated being tethered to a hospital bed when Leah was free to go about her business. If his mental radar was working correctly, her "business" probably involved his own physician.

"You also," she continued, "aren't in a position to fend for yourself. Taking a shower completely wore you out. How will you function on your own?"

"I'll manage," he said, unwilling to spring his plan on her just yet.

Now she looked exasperated. "Fine. Do whatever you want, regardless of what your doctor or anyone else suggests. Frankly, with your attitude, I'm surprised you bothered coming to the hospital at all for medical attention."

Her comment struck home as he realized she was right. He *had* gotten to the point where he assessed a situation and made a decision without asking for advice or input, and if any was given contrary to his opinion, he didn't follow it.

The question was, had he always been that way? He truly didn't think so. At one time he hadn't been able to wait to share everything in his day with her and he hadn't made any plans without consulting her first, but now that he thought about it, that aspect of their life had changed after they'd lost both babies. Granted, the second child hadn't died, but when the birth mother had taken her daughter home instead of putting her in their care, it had felt the same.

Conversation had dwindled when she'd been grieving and although he'd tried to get his feelings out in the open, he'd soon given up. Leah's sorrow had been so overwhelming he hadn't wanted to burden her with his own pain, so he'd bottled his emotions and carried on.

Instead of coping together, they'd coped separately. He'd focused on his job and expanding the foundation's services while she'd flung herself first into a remodeling project and then into her job at the hospital. Eventually, their diverging interests had allowed them to drift apart until their marriage had reached breaking point.

He should have done things differently but he hadn't. Fate, however, had given him another chance and he was determined to make the most of it. The first step, however, was to prove that he *was* listening and valuing her opinion, even if her opinion conflicted with his own wishes.

"If you want me to stay, then I'll stay, but only on an outpatient basis until tomorrow morning," he qualified.

"I can live with that," Jeff immediately agreed, as if he realized this compromise wouldn't remain on the table for long.

Gabe continued, "And only if Leah is my nurse. My private nurse."

Leah's jaw dropped, plainly surprised he'd included her as part of his conditional surrender. A moment later, her expression cleared. "I cover the ED, not this ward," she pointed out, somewhat smugly.

He steadily met his colleague's gaze. "Jeff?"

The other physician pressed his lips together, then nodded. "If she's what it will take to keep you in that bed, I'll work it out," he promised.

Leah's jaw immediately closed with a decided snap, her eyes flashing fire. It was a small victory and one that she clearly didn't support, so Gabe forced himself not to smile. As compromises went, he'd gained more than he'd expected, although it was less than he'd wanted. What really felt good, though, was finally seeing Leah with her normal spark instead of appearing as if all the life had been sucked out of her.

"Fine," she said a trifle waspishly, "but I'm adding a condition, too. You'll stay until he releases you."

"Okay, but he *will* release me tomorrow morning." He glanced at his colleague. "Won't you, Jeff?"

Jeff appeared more interested in the tug-of-war between Leah and Gabe than in Gabe's capitulation. "If nothing horrible shows up on your cultures and you don't spike any fevers, then you have my word you'll be out of here in twenty-four hours."

Gabe leaned his head against the pillows, too exhausted to complain about how their final agreement had as many exemptions as a bill before Congress. He'd face those scenarios when and if he had to. "I want to know everything the minute you do."

"I wouldn't expect otherwise." Jeff addressed Leah. "In the meantime, good luck with your patient."

Gabe tried not to be jealous of how easily she smiled at his colleague—his divorced, *single* colleague—the same divorced colleague who'd probably been more than happy to comfort Leah during the past year, especially during the month after he'd been presumed dead. However, jealousy was a good thing, he decided, because it gave him added incentive to win her back again.

"Not to worry," she said airily. "If he misbehaves, I have a sedative with his name on it."

"I'd rather eat a steak, medium-well, with baked potato," Gabe said as he eyed the tray of food Leah had organized from the unit's kitchenette.

A steaming bowl of chicken broth with assorted crackers, strawberry and lime gelatin squares, and chocolate pudding were the result of her raid.

"Maybe you'll get those for dinner tonight," Leah said lightly, knowing he wouldn't. As much as she'd like to reverse his weight loss as quickly as possible, his digestive system needed to acclimate first. "This is just a snack until then."

"There's nothing here for a man to sink his teeth into."

She ignored his grumbling as she studied his skin tone with clinical detachment. Now that he'd scraped off his beard with the disposable razor she'd provided, he was paler than she'd like. His face, although still handsome with his straight nose and strong chin, was thinner and his cheekbones more pronounced than the last time she'd seen him.

"For good reason," she answered. "You hardly have the strength to chew."

"I can find the energy if it's worth my while," he said. "A cheeseburger, fries and a milkshake would—"

"Come up as fast as they went down. Would you rather hug the toilet for a few hours? Now, just try this," she wheedled. "If your system can handle this without any problems, I'll personally deliver a greasy cheeseburger from your favorite fast-food restaurant later on."

His sigh was loud enough to be heard in the hallway, but he picked up a package of crackers. After struggling unsuccessfully to tear the Cellophane, he finally gave up and tossed the packet of crumbs onto the tray in disgust.

"Would you like me to open it?" she asked, reaching for the mangled package.

Hating to admit his weakness, he grimaced. "I changed my mind. A fellow can do that, can't he?"

"Of course you can," she soothed, aware of the hit the tiny packet had leveled against his dignity. It was also clear that her time in the kitchen would be wasted if she didn't take matters into her own hands, so she picked up the spoon and began feeding him soup.

"I can do this myself," he protested between swallows.

She doubted it. He was clearly exhausted from the poking and prodding, the round of X-rays and his stint in the shower, but for some reason he refused to sleep. Maybe a full stomach would work for him as well as it did for babies.

"I know," she agreed, "but I'm trying to earn my pay. I am your nurse, remember?"

It still rankled how Jeff had marched into the nursing vice president's office and when he'd come out again, it was official. Leah was assigned to one patient and one patient only—Gabriel Montgomery.

"'This is all so pointless," she had railed at the emergency physician. "Gabe doesn't need nursing care. He only needs someone to fetch and carry and help him in and out of bed, and anyone can do that. He doesn't need me and I can't believe you agreed to this. We have a date coming up!"

"I did it *because* of our date," Jeff had told her kindly. "You've been riding an emotional roller coaster for the past few weeks. Now that he's back, you need to rethink exactly what you want—"

"I *know* what I want," she'd interrupted.

"You *think* you know what you want," he'd corrected, "but having Gabe return from the dead changes everything."

"It doesn't," she'd insisted, trying to convince herself as much as him.

Jeff had smiled benevolently at her. "It may not, but you owe it to yourself, and to me, to be absolutely certain of what you're looking for in a relationship. But I'll be honest," he'd said as he'd squeezed her shoulder. "As much as I respect Gabe, I won't be rooting for him."

And so she'd accepted the inevitable, even though she believed her skills were being wasted and that she knew her own mind when it came to her broken marriage.

Yet, after it had taken all of her concentration to reel her thoughts in far enough to figure out the microwave controls to heat his broth, she had to admit that perhaps she *shouldn't* be working in the ED right now. While she felt guilty over leaving her department short-handed, she shuddered to think of how ineffective she'd be in handling a trauma victim when a life hung in the balance. To her utter disgust, feeding Gabe seemed to be the only task her jumbled mind could handle.

"Are you ready to try the gelatin?" she asked, spooning a red cube into his mouth before he could refuse.

He swallowed. "Do you work with Jeff often?"

"Usually. Like I said, I normally work in Emergency."

His brow furrowed. "Don't PRN nurses work everywhere in the hospital?"

She spooned another bite into his mouth. "Some do, some don't. I haven't since I completed my advanced trauma nursing coursework six months ago."

His brow furrowed. "I didn't know that."

"You didn't notice the nursing textbooks on the coffee table before I moved out?"

"I did, but I thought you were boning up because you'd accepted this relief position."

"I was. Then I decided to take the next step." She hesitated, realizing that while he could have asked, she also should have volunteered the information. Now she wondered if the reason she hadn't said anything had been because she'd wanted *him* to notice and express an interest in what she was doing. And when he hadn't, she'd counted it as a strike against him.

"I should have told you," she said.

He shrugged. "We both had problems with communication, didn't we?"

At least he wasn't putting the burden all on her and if he could be magnanimous, so could she. "To be fair," she began slowly, "some of your staff had quit and you were trying to take up the slack. You had larger problems than wondering why textbooks had appeared on the table. More gelatin?"

He shook his head, his gaze intent. "Are you working full time?"

"Officially, no. Unofficially, yes, but I'm not reaping the benefits," she said ruefully. "However, the director of nursing told me yesterday that the next available position will be mine." She shoved another gelatin cube in his mouth.

He chewed, swallowed, then surprised her with his next question. "How was your cousin's wedding?"

She froze. "You knew about Angela's wedding?"

"She sent me an invitation. I would have gone, but I didn't want to make the day awkward for you. Things will be different, though, for your next family function."

Different? "Excuse me?"

"I want us to save our marriage, Leah. To fix what went wrong with our relationship."

At one time those were words she'd dreamt he would say, but too much time had passed. He was asking for the impossible.

"I know you went through a traumatic experience," she said slowly, "and as a result you want to right the perceived wrongs in your life as part of whatever foxhole conversion you experienced, but what happened to us—to me—can't be fixed."

"It can," he insisted.

"Not if our relationship is tied to my medical history."

"It isn't."

She raised an eyebrow because, to her, it was. "Oh?"

"It never was."

She eyed him carefully. "Maybe I should have Jeff order a CT scan because I think you suffered a concussion. In case you've forgotten, our relationship began its downhill slope when I lost Andrew and any chance for more children."

"It may have, but we can turn our life around. Children or not, we can make our marriage into whatever we want it to be."

His fierce determination was almost contagious, but his rhetoric didn't change one important fact. This man, who should have gone into pediatrics because he loved little people, was destined to remain childless because she refused to risk another adoptive mother changing her mind in the final hour. And he'd made it quite plain over the years that his biggest wish was to fill his house with children—children she couldn't give him, whether they were his or someone else's.

Neither did his sincerity change the fact that his work at the foundation was probably far more rewarding than simply coming home to her each night. And, yes, she could join him on his trips as she had when they were first married and she'd rearranged her hospital schedule, but deep down she was a homebody while he was a traveler. Eventually, the difference would become an issue again.

"For what it's worth, I *am* glad you're back," she said simply, "but now isn't the time to discuss what went wrong in our life." She rose to push his bedside table away. "Your only concern should be to give yourself time to heal."

He frowned, clearly not liking her response. "I can't believe you're giving up on us so easily."

"To you, I'm giving up, but to me, I'm finally putting the past behind me. Which is what you should be doing, too."

He paused. "How long have you been seeing Jeff?"

She froze, startled by his question. "Jeff? I'm not... We haven't... We're just friends," she finished lamely, wondering how Gabe had drawn that particular conclusion when she'd been so careful to hide her burgeoning interest in the other man.

"But you'd like it to be more."

"You're guessing," she countered, hating it that he could read her so well.

He shrugged. "I saw the way he looked at you. I only want to know what I'm up against."

She didn't know why she felt compelled to explain, but she did. "We went for a beer a few times with the rest of the ED crowd on a Friday night, but nothing more than that. You and I may have lived apart, but I still took my wedding vows seriously, which was why I was waiting to pursue a relationship with Jeff until after…"

"After I signed the divorce papers?" he finished.

"Yes."

"But once you heard my plane had crashed, you didn't need them. Why didn't you two take things to the next level right away?"

He sounded more curious than argumentative, so she answered as honestly as she could.

"If you must know, I wanted to wait until after the foundation's annual fund-raiser. I'd already decided it would be my last one—and it seemed appropriate for our chapter to end there. Now that you're back, there isn't any point in waiting, is there?"

He paused. "Is that what you want? For me to sign your papers?"

Was that what she wanted? Perhaps if their differences weren't irreconcilable, perhaps if they hadn't grown apart, perhaps if Gabe treated their marriage as a partnership rather than a boss-employee relationship, she could risk giving him another chance, but she couldn't.

"While I'm thrilled you aren't dead," she said softly, "you have to admit we're better off apart than we are together."

"I disagree."

"How can you say that?"

"Because we've *been* apart and it hasn't worked for me. I've missed you, Leah. More than you can imagine."

"How is that possible?" she asked, more curious than cynical. "You were busy with your work. We rarely talked or saw each other."

"That doesn't mean I didn't miss the days when we *did* talk and I spent more time at home than any place else. I want us to reverse course. To go back to the way we were. Before everything happened."

Before everything happened—such a polite way of saying *before her world went to hell in a handbasket.*

Her mind's eye flashed to the nursery they'd prepared on two separate occasions. The same room that remained closed to everyone except the housekeeper who periodically dusted and vacuumed. The sore spot in her heart had lessened from the day she'd given up and finally locked the door, but it hadn't completely disappeared. Her plans to avoid the OB and nursery wing were proof of that.

"As great as the idea sounds, I don't know if we can," she said honestly. "We aren't the same starry-eyed people we once were and no amount of magical fairy dust will change us back."

He tugged her arm until she didn't have a choice but to perch on the edge of his bed. "Maybe we aren't the young, naive kids we once were. Maybe the hopes and dreams we once had died, but that doesn't mean we can't create new ones. Together."

Darn it, but his grip was comforting and once again his voice was so sincere—so full of faith—that the wall she'd created in her heart to hold back her hurts and disappointments began to crumble. Quickly, she struggled to shore up those widening cracks before those emotions overwhelmed her.

"Life has seasoned us," he continued softly, "but deep down, we're the same two people who fell in love. Getting ourselves back on track won't be easy and won't happen overnight, but anything worth having is worth fighting for. I've had weeks to do nothing *but* think and I'm asking you to not give up on me or on us." He paused to caress her hand. "Please."

Once again, he'd surprised her. He could have so easily *demanded* this of her, but instead he'd spoken in a humble manner. Maybe Gabe *had* experienced a change of heart…. However, as he'd said, he'd had the luxury of time to think about their life while she had not.

"I love you, Leah," he added hoarsely. "I want another chance."

As his words soaked in, tears sprang into her eyes and the wall inside her completely gave way. Instead of being happy, she felt angry.

She jerked her hand out of his and rose as she clenched her fists and stuffed them into her pockets.

"What's wrong?" he asked, his gaze puzzled as he followed her retreat to the opposite end of the room. "I thought you'd be thrilled—"

"Do you know…?" She fought the tears clogging her throat. "Do you know how long…it's been…since you told me that?"

"Judging from your response, longer than I thought," he said wryly.

"I'll say. And I had to wait to hear it until after you were nearly killed in a plane crash! You can't spring that on me, out of the blue." She watched him struggle to swing his legs off the edge of the bed. "What are you doing?"

"I'm getting up," he said as he put action to his words.

"You can't. Your IV—"

"To hell with my IV," he said fiercely as his first step toward her pulled the tubing taut.

Fearing he'd rip out the needle and undo her hard work, she hurried close to survey his hand for signs of damage. She'd taped everything down to avoid accidental dislodging, but tape wasn't a deterrent to a man determined to escape his tether. "What are you trying to do?"

"I'm trying to get to my wife."

Before she could move, she found herself pulled into his

embrace. She resisted at first, but the moment his arms surrounded her, she realized this was where she wanted to be.
Oh, how she'd missed times like this, when they'd simply
been happy to hold each other for no reason, other than "just
because".

He kissed her forehead before pressing his cheek against
hers. "I'm sorry," he murmured, "but everything is going to
be okay."

She didn't answer because she didn't believe it to be true.
How could it? So much had happened, so much had been lost,
and they couldn't regain any of it. Then, after she'd reflected
on the bittersweet moment, she pulled away and cleared her
throat.

"You'd better get back into bed," she fussed, falling into
her nurse persona as she avoided his gaze.

He didn't quibble but simply allowed her to help him sink
onto the mattress, which spoke of how much his gesture had
cost him. "I liked where I was," he said instead as she covered
his legs with the blanket.

How could she answer? She had enjoyed his embrace, too,
but she shouldn't. She'd wanted a divorce, for heaven's sake!
Ending their marriage was the only solution because she could
no longer define their relationship. Were they friends or en-
emies, or just two hurting people who'd lived together until
she'd realized the status quo wasn't enough? Did she still have
feelings for him or was she just falling into old habits because
she was relieved that he hadn't died? Did she respond because
of those feelings, or because it had been so very long since
someone had comforted her or held her in his arms?

"Didn't you?" he pressed.

She hadn't followed his conversation because she'd been
so caught up in trying to answer her own questions. "Didn't
I what?"

"Like where you were?"

Knowing his tendency toward persistence—he wouldn't
stop asking until she answered—she intended to deny her
feelings until she met his gaze. To her surprise, she didn't see

a smirk or satisfaction in those dark depths. Instead, she saw hesitation and uncertainty.

Her strong, silent, take-charge husband suffered from the same doubts and insecurities she did, and she'd never noticed until now.

"Come on, Leah," he coaxed. "Talk to me."

"If I tell you the truth, will you hush and rest?"

He nodded.

"Yes, I enjoyed where I was, but—" she injected a firm note into her voice "—that doesn't mean anything. It can't."

"Because you still want a divorce."

She didn't necessarily *want* one; she simply didn't have any other option. "It's for the best," she prevaricated.

He fell silent. "Okay, then," he said. "I'll sign your papers."

CHAPTER FOUR

GABE looked on as Leah stared at him in mute surprise. Clearly, she hadn't expected him to give in so readily. "You will?" she finally asked.

"Yes, but I have some conditions."

One corner of her kissable mouth turned up in disgust. "Naturally. And they are?"

"We move back in together first and see if we can make our marriage work."

"No."

"It's the only way I'll sign."

She opened her mouth then snapped it closed before she glared at him. "This is blackmail."

"It's negotiation," he countered.

"Your idea is pointless."

"We'll never know if we don't try. Whatever we do, don't you want to be sure, absolutely *certain*, that we're doing the right thing?"

"I'm already certain," she told him. "I was certain weeks ago, when I came by and delivered that folder of documents."

"Well, I'm not." He softened his tone. "Come on, Leah. If you're so certain, think of this as your opportunity to convince me it's the right thing to do."

"We don't need to live together for me to convince you."

"Maybe not, but it's one of my conditions."

"*But—*"

"Next," he interrupted her to add, "we have to really *try* to heal our marriage. Not simply live together like we did before, as married singles with each of us going our own way. We'll spend time together and we'll talk. No more overworking, no more avoiding our emotions or minimizing our feelings. We say what we mean and we mean what we say. And if we can't open up to each other, we'll go to a professional counselor."

She fell silent and Gabe hardly breathed as he waited for her answer. "Is that a condition, too?"

He nodded. "We'll definitely fail if the effort is one-sided or if we focus on the negatives instead of the positives. Surely you can invest a few weeks to salvage a ten-year marriage?"

"And who's to say one of us isn't working 'hard enough'." She made quotation marks in the air.

"If you think I'm not holding up my part of the bargain, you have to say so. I'll do the same."

Once again, she hesitated. "How long do you want this ridic—this exercise to last?"

He had a feeling she'd intended to call his trial run "ridiculous" but the fact that she'd corrected her negative remark suggested she was warming ever so slightly to the idea. "Until the foundation ball."

"Six weeks?" she sputtered. "No. Impossible."

"Are you afraid?"

"Absolutely not. I'm objecting because six weeks is a long time to prolong the inevitable."

"Six weeks will pass by in a flash. As for the outcome being inevitable, maybe it is and maybe it isn't, but if you quit one day short of our agreement, I won't sign the papers," he warned. "We'll end up with the messiest divorce in state history."

Dividing their property wouldn't be the problem. Leah hadn't been interested in his family money and hadn't touched a dime in the account he'd created for her after she'd moved out. Her Achilles' heel was the notoriety and publicity associated with divorcing the heir to the Montgomery fortune. And from the resignation in her eyes, she realized he could turn their divorce into a headline or a simple record on the district court blotter.

"You aren't playing fair," she complained. "A month should be more than enough."

"Oh, I don't know. Six weeks doesn't seem like very long when you'll have the rest of your life to spend with Jeff, or anyone else for that matter."

Her shoulders slumped in obvious capitulation. "I suppose not."

"There's also one more thing."

She rolled her eyes. "Why am I not surprised?"

"I want you to go with me when I head to Ciuflores, Mexico, in three days."

"What?" she screeched. "You're going back to Mexico, and you want me to go with you?"

"Yes."

"That settles it," she said firmly. "You definitely need a CT scan. Heck, probably a neurologist."

"My head is fine."

"Fine or not," she snapped, "my answer is no. Absolutely *no*."

He shrugged, as if unfazed by her outburst or her objection. "Then no signature."

"Why in the world would you want to go on another trip?" she asked, clearly ignoring his comment. "You barely came back alive from the last one. You should be giving yourself time to recover, not rushing to jet around the world again."

"In three days, I'll have recovered."

"No one heals from cracked ribs that quickly. You'll be sore and bruised. And you'll still need antibiotics for your leg, too."

"I'll take the antibiotics with me. And with you there to make sure I take them I'll be fine."

"Fine or not, why you, Gabe? You can't be the only member of the Montgomery Foundation who can travel."

"No, I'm not, but Sheldon told me just before you came in with my lunch that Father David had called and asked for supplies. They're in the middle of a flu epidemic and the situation is dire. I can't refuse his request—he's my friend."

Father David Odell was Gabe's old schoolfriend and although they'd taken different paths in life, they'd kept in contact. For the past few years David had served as the spiritual advisor to a poor community and had been instrumental in introducing Gabe to the two physicians who were the sole medical providers in the remote area. It hadn't taken long for the local doctors to recognize the advantages being handed to them through the generosity of the Montgomery Medical Foundation. Eventually, Gabe had arranged for the tele-medicine link for which his organization was famous, and two months ago he'd delivered the equipment and trained the staff on its use.

"Fine. If you want to go, then go. But I'm—"

"I need you, Leah," he said simply. "The people of Ciuflores need you. An extra pair of medically trained hands is in as much demand as anything I can supply."

She rubbed the back of her neck in obvious indecision and he pressed on. "There was a time when you couldn't wait to go on one of my trips," he reminded her. "And if I recall, you loved the experience."

"Yes, but I have responsibilities of my own here," she argued.

"I've checked out your work commitments and I know that as of today you're officially off the work schedule for the next ten days," he said. "Plenty of time to go on a three-day mission of mercy."

"And what comes after that? There's always another deserving community waiting in the wings."

"Not for me," he said firmly. "Oh, I may go places once or twice a year, but for the most part my traveling days will be over."

"Oh, please," she scoffed.

"I don't mind if you're skeptical. I would be too if I were in your shoes, but it's true. Saving our marriage requires time and proximity." He paused. "Is it a deal?"

"When does this unholy pact start?"

"Tomorrow. As soon as we get home."

"And in six weeks, when you finally accept that we're incompatible, you'll sign the papers, no arguments?"

There was no way they were incompatible—they'd had too many good years together—but if she wanted to think their time together would prove it, then she could. He, on the other hand, intended to show her just how *compatible* they really were.

"No arguments," he said, "but this is an all-out effort on both our parts. No halfhearted attempts at reconciliation. We give it our best shot." He knew he was repeating himself, but he wanted the terms perfectly clear. She wouldn't be able to cry foul down the road.

She let out an exasperated sigh. "Fine. Then you'd better get some rest tonight. Tomorrow will be an extremely busy day for both of us."

Physically he was exhausted, but emotionally he felt as if he could move mountains. He'd gotten Leah to agree to one last-ditch effort to save their marriage and with far less effort and cajolery than he'd expected. He wanted to believe that she'd given in because she wasn't quite as convinced about her plan as she'd originally let on but, whatever the reason, he was getting his second chance and he intended to make the most of it.

He'd handled things poorly before and now, after replaying those scenes and imagining ways he should have acted differently, he could straighten out those kinks. He'd start with sharing his own fears and feelings instead of hiding them behind his work. Hopefully, time had faded enough of Leah's hurts so he wouldn't feel guilty for dumping his own pain on top of hers. His father had taught him to be tough at all costs, but in this case the lessons he'd learned had come at the expense of his marriage.

"Okay, but—"

She held a hand in the air. "We've talked enough for now. Get some sleep."

He'd pushed all he dared, but he'd gotten more than he'd expected on his first try. Even so, he was curious...

"Why are you so eager for me to doze off?" he asked as she adjusted his bedding once more. Her actions were completely unnecessary because there wasn't a wrinkle in sight.

"Gabe," she chided. "People sleep while they're in the hospital. Rest is part of every patient's treatment plan."

"What will you do?"

"I'll think of something."

"You won't leave?" He hated the plaintive note in his voice, but he'd awakened far too often to the disappointing discovery that Leah's presence had only been a dream.

"I'll be here when you wake up."

"Promise?" he asked, hiding his worry behind a light-hearted tone.

She nodded, offering him a slight smile. "I promise."

"Ramon! Hold on!"

Gabe's rising voice and restless movements brought Leah out of her catnap. As she had done so many times during the last twelve hours, she padded across the dark room to pull him out of his nightmare.

"It's okay," she repeated as she sat in the chair next to his bed and held his free hand. "It's only a dream."

"I'm sorry," he murmured, still in the grip of his memories. "'Sall my fault." Then, "Not Will, too!"

His anguish was almost palpable and all Leah could do was watch him relive those moments of horror with tears in her own eyes.

"So sorry, guys," he murmured as tears slipped out from behind his closed eyes and his shoulders shook. "So sorry. My fault. All my fault."

Slowly, he settled back into his uneasy slumber, although she didn't know if her voice or her touch had caused that particular scene to fade.

Oh, Gabe. You went through hell, didn't you?

As she lightly blotted the moisture from his face with a

damp washcloth, stroked the hard lines of his cheekbones and brushed aside the lock of hair on his sweaty forehead, she murmured what had become her litany. Idly, she wondered if Jack and Theresa were reliving their horrible memories, too. No doubt they were. Poor Theresa.

With his face freshened, she continued to hold his hand and stroke his fingers, thinking about how he'd glossed over his experience to her, to Jeff, and probably to everyone else he'd spoken to since he'd returned. Now, though, in the dark of night and without his full awareness, he'd given her a glimpse of the tragedy and trauma he'd endured.

She'd been so caught up in having him home again and worrying over what his return meant to her personally that she hadn't considered the emotional aftermath of his experience. For the past two years she'd thought him cold, unfeeling and insensitive, but he'd obviously been more adept at hiding his emotions, compartmentalizing his feelings and carrying on in the face of adversity and disappointment than she was.

Worse, though, was how, as a nurse, she should have *known* he would feel survivor's guilt, not only because he'd lived through his ordeal and his friends had not but also because *his* organization had been responsible for sending them on this trip in the first place.

No wonder he felt as if he were to blame.

He should have told her all this, she thought self-righteously, but almost immediately she understood why he hadn't. He couldn't blurt out the whole traumatic tale the moment he saw her, could he, especially when they'd lived separate lives for a year? Ever since they'd been reunited, they'd been surrounded by people and hadn't had the time or the privacy to delve into the details.

Had that been the problem with their own losses? Had they been surrounded by so many well-meaning friends and family that they'd never had the opportunity to deal with their pain as a couple? And when they'd tried, had they both buried it so far underground that they hadn't been able to reach it?

As she gazed at his face and smoothed away the agony

etched there, his vulnerability tugged on her heartstrings. No, she decided, she felt more than compassion for a traumatized patient. She felt the pain of seeing a loved one suffer.

A *former* loved one, she amended. She didn't love Gabe in the same eye-sparkling, heart-racing way she once had because there were too many hurts and philosophical differences between them, but underneath all the bad stuff, the stuff that had gone wrong, the affection they'd once shared was there.

Unfortunately, affection didn't make a marriage. Love did, and hers had faded. Gabe might think they could rekindle those feelings but even if that were possible, he'd still want the family she couldn't give him. And as she'd told her mother when she'd phoned her earlier in the evening to share the news of Gabe's miraculous return, eventually they'd wind up in the same untenable situation.

Her mother hadn't been as certain about the outcome as she was but with Gabe's parents having died years earlier—one in a car accident and the other of a heart attack—her mom had always carried a soft spot in her heart for her son-in-law. While she was willing to support Leah's decision, whatever it might be, she'd also thought Gabe's suggestion made sense.

Clearly, everyone was hoping she and Gabe would have a happy ending, although Leah had given up believing in them.

But happy ending or not, she'd made a deal in order to win the prize she wanted—his name scrawled across the bottom of legal papers. In the meantime, she'd follow the letter of their verbal contract. "Say what you mean and mean what you say," he'd said, and she intended to live by that rule.

Perhaps the best place to begin was with the deaths of his friends. Their loss obviously weighed heavily on him and if he would express his feelings openly on that subject, perhaps they could work their way into dealing with their personal issues.

Relieved he was finally resting easier, she stifled a yawn. She should go back to her recliner, but decided she didn't have the strength or the desire to let go of his hand. Perhaps it was wishful thinking on her part, but it seemed as if this small contact was enough to hold his nightmares at bay.

She'd never felt as if Gabe had needed her, but in this, at least, he apparently did. For now, it was enough.

Gabe drifted awake to find the sun shining through the half-opened mini-blinds covering his window. Leah stood in the sunlight, gazing into the courtyard, arms crossed, her brow furrowed as if contemplating a serious subject.

For a moment, he simply lay there, looking his fill. They'd lost so much these past few years and, if not for his accident, they might have continued down their separate paths to an irreparable end. In fact, during the first few days of his trip, he'd seriously considered agreeing to her suggestion of a divorce, not because he wanted one but because he'd felt like such a failure. After being unable to give Leah her heart's desire—a baby—in this, at least, he could give her something she wanted.

The plane crash, however, had changed everything.

As he stared at his wife, who was more beautiful now than she had been when they'd married, he knew he would do everything in his power to make her happy again.

Suddenly, she faced him and smiled, looking more relaxed than she had a minute ago. "You're awake," she said.

"Hello to you, too," he said, his voice rusty from disuse.

She approached his bed, clearly intent on his IV pump, but he reached out and snagged her hand. Her hand was soft, her bone structure fine and her eyes uncertain.

Gabe, however, had no doubts, no reservations about what he wanted. He tugged her just hard enough to shift her center of gravity in his direction.

"Gabe," she protested.

Before she could utter another word, he tipped his chin to meet her mouth. Gradually, her lips softened under his and a small noise escaped her mouth—the same small sound that came out as a satisfied sigh.

He wished he could give her the sort of kiss he wanted to, but he didn't want fuzzy-teeth breath when he did. "Good morning," he whispered.

"Same to you," she answered, her voice as husky as he remembered from their more lighthearted days. Then, as if she recalled where she was, she straightened and began fiddling with his tubing. "How do you feel?"

The nurse was back and the bride he remembered had vanished. No matter. There would be time to find her again—just as soon as he sprang himself from this joint.

He took stock of his aches and pains. They were still there, and a few new ones had cropped up, but his bone-weary exhaustion was gone. "Pretty good. How about you?"

"Me?" She seemed startled by his question. "I'm fine."

"I wondered. From your expression as you were staring out the window, I'd guess you were solving the world's problems," he said offhandedly.

She disconnected the tubing from the cannula in his wrist and draped it over the IV stand. "Not the world's, just the foundation banquet's."

"What's wrong?" he asked.

"Sheldon and I had planned a memorial ceremony, but with your return we should turn it into a celebration."

"Keep the memorial idea," he advised. "It doesn't seem right to celebrate when two of my group didn't come home."

"Okay, but your friends, associates and donors will want to hear about your experiences. You intend to speak as usual, don't you?"

"Only briefly," he said. "I'd rather review the year in pictures."

"Then we will." She flicked his blankets off his feet. "Are you ready for a stroll to the bathroom?"

"I thought you'd never ask," he said fervently as he levered himself up with his good arm and swung his legs off the edge of the bed.

"Take it slow," she advised. "You're probably stiff and sore."

Every muscle ached and his ribs protested his movements but he ignored the pain as he hobbled across the room to his destination, aware of his wife hovering beside him in case he should fall en route. "No kidding, I can manage from here."

He closed the door for privacy to take care of his most pressing needs. Then he studied his face in the mirror and rubbed at the stubble before proceeding to remove it.

Fifteen minutes later, he left the bathroom and found a meal tray waiting on his bedside table. "I'd rather eat at home," he said.

"Good luck with that," she said. "I emptied your refrigerator and pantry a few weeks ago when we thought you weren't coming...back. By the time we shop for necessities, it will be well past lunchtime. Besides, if you don't eat this, this delicious hospital cafeteria cuisine will only go to waste."

"Is that what you're calling it these days to make it taste good? *Cuisine*?"

"How did you guess?"

"You can have it," he offered.

"Sorry. You need the nutrition more than I do."

"Then I'll share. Remember when we shared a piece of pie?"

She smiled. "That was only so I could appease my sweet tooth at a fraction of the calories. This, however, is a *healthy* meal and you need to eat every bite. You should be starved."

"I am a little hungry."

"I would think so. You haven't eaten since the soup and crackers I'd fixed for you yesterday afternoon, so dig in before your eggs get cold."

"Okay, okay," he groused as he headed for the chair, "but I'll sit in the recliner. Lolling in bed makes me feel like I'm sick and I'm not."

"No, you're not," she said. "How did you sleep?"

He vaguely remembered her unhooking his IV before stumbling to the bathroom at some point, but other than the occasional murmur of Leah's voice, there was nothing he could focus on.

"Fine, I guess," he said slowly, watching as she whipped the stainless-steel dome off his plate to reveal several strips of bacon, two generous scoops of scrambled eggs and four pieces of buttered toast. "I can't believe I missed dinner, though. Eating is something we all looked forward to. Jack kept talking about his famous grilled chicken and Theresa wanted anything covered in chocolate."

"And what did you want?"

"Your Irish stew. Any chance we can have that one night?" he asked as he dug into the eggs and decided they didn't taste like hospital cooking. However, if she expected him to polish off the double portion, she'd be sorely disappointed.

"I'll see what I can do. Maybe I'll work on it while you're napping this afternoon."

He shook his head as he chewed. "If I nap, I won't be able to sleep tonight."

"You might surprise yourself. Being at home, in your own bed can make a big difference with how well you sleep."

Something in her tone put him on alert. Worry over what he might have said knotted his stomach. "I had a nightmare, didn't I?"

"It was pretty intense. Do you have bad dreams every night?"

He carefully placed his fork on his plate, his appetite gone. "At first, yes. The last week or so, not as often. I'd hoped they'd disappear once I got home."

"Would you like to talk about it?"

He let out a deep breath. "No," he said honestly. Then, because he noticed her stiffen, he finished his sentence. "But I should."

"You said we have to be more open and express our thoughts and feelings," she reminded him. "It's part of our contract."

"I know, and I will. The problem is, I don't know where

to begin." He pushed his plate back. "Here. I'm not hungry anymore."

She bit her lower lip, clearly not happy with his answer or his sudden loss of appetite, but she simply nodded. "Too much too soon?"

He wondered if she was asking about the food or the conversation, but he didn't press for clarification. "Yes," he admitted.

"Small meals more often is probably best."

She'd been talking about food, which was a relief. "Probably," he said.

"The same holds true for our conversation. Even if you can't share everything all at once, a little bit here and there is better than holding it all inside."

She'd caught him off guard, but her analogy was sound. He let out a deep breath. "I know."

"Good, because I'll let you slide this time, but once we're home, the kid gloves come off," she told him.

Relieved by his reprieve, he nodded. "I wouldn't have it any other way. By the way, when can I leave?"

"As soon as you have another blood test," she said. "In fact, someone from the lab should be here shortly."

As if on cue, there came a knock at the door and it was, as Leah had predicted, a phlebotomist. A few minutes later, the woman left with her vials and Gabe opted to enjoy the shower once again.

This time, when he came out of the bathroom, he felt like a new man and said so.

"You certainly look better than you did when you first arrived," she responded.

"I had nowhere to go but up," he quipped.

"On the contrary, you could have gotten worse," she said sternly, as if he needed the reminder. "Thanks to your overnight stay and the miracle of antibiotics, the redness on your leg has faded a lot already. I'm sure your ribs benefitted from the rest, too."

"Maybe so, but—"

"Jeff was right and you know it," she insisted. "In fact, if your roles had been reversed, you would have done the same."

"Okay, okay. I'll cry uncle. But I know Jeff has designs on you so don't expect me to praise him as if he's the next Albert Schweitzer."

The sound of her laughter caught him by surprise. It had seemed like forever since he'd heard it. "What's so funny?" he asked.

"You." She smiled. "You're jealous."

"Of course," he said smoothly. "I'm not embarrassed to admit it, either, especially when the prettiest woman in the hospital is my wife."

At first, she appeared taken aback, then a pink hue colored her skin, which suggested that he was long overdue when it came to paying compliments and giving attention to his spouse. He'd fallen down in that area, too, but that was another mistake he planned to correct.

Although, as he studied her, he noticed a few other details, too. Details like wrinkled scrubs, dark smudges under her eyes and an occasional stifled yawn.

"Did you stay here all night?" he asked, guessing her answer.

"I said I would."

"I can't believe you didn't go home."

"I didn't know when you'd wake up," she said simply, "and I promised I'd be here when you did."

The fact that she'd put her own comfort aside and gone to such lengths for him when he didn't deserve it was humbling.

"While I appreciate your gesture, you should have left at some point to get some rest," he chided.

"I should have," she agreed. "If I'd known your nap would stretch into eighteen hours, I would have."

"Why didn't you?"

"Glutton for punishment," she said lightly. "By the way, you had a steady stream of visitors, so I made a list because I didn't want to forget anyone." She grabbed the yellow steno pad lying on the table and held it out. "Would you like to…?"

He waved her offer aside. "I'll read it later."

"Sheldon came by several times. He insisted you call him the minute you're awake."

"He can wait."

"He won't be happy," she warned.

"I'll see him soon enough." He glanced at the wall clock. "Any chance you can call the lab and get my report?"

"Impatient as usual."

"If I have to sit and do nothing, I'd rather—"

"Sit and do nothing at home," she finished for him.

He grinned sheepishly. "I've said that before, haven't I?"

"Yeah, but you'll have to hold tight for a few minutes while I pester the lab for the results."

"Okay, but don't forget I want to see the report, too."

"As if you'd let me forget," she answered wryly, before she slipped out of the room.

CHAPTER FIVE

GABE found a pair of loose-fitting chinos and a button-down shirt in the tiny closet and decided to beat the proverbial rush and change now rather than later. He unhooked his IV, leaving the cannula in his arm for Leah to deal with, then slowly dressed. The process wasn't pain free by any means, but his struggles only gave him another good reason for needing Leah at home with him.

He was sitting on the edge of his bed, waiting for the sharp pain in his ribs to fade, when Dr. Taylor Ewing strolled in.

"How are you, Gabe?" the chief of surgery asked in his booming voice.

"Doing better now that I'm home," Gabe answered.

"Good, good. Getting dismissed soon, I take it?"

"As soon as my latest blood test is done."

"In that case, before you go, would you mind reviewing a case? It came via email through your medical organization and as it's my first official foray into your world of telemedicine, I'd like you watching over my shoulder. I'd hate to delete a crucial file by accident."

Gabe had signed Taylor as a consultant in exchange for filling in as a surgeon when the department was short-staffed. The arrangement had been in both of their best interests. It gave Gabe a break from his organization's administrative duties and kept his surgical skills from growing rusty. Not that becoming rusty was a problem…when he and his staff were invited into an area with their supplies and equipment, they often assisted the local medical community.

"Who's asking for a consult?" he asked.

"A Dr. Hector Aznar."

Hector was one of the two Ciuflores physicians Gabe had come to know quite well. He and his partner, Miguel Diego, were dedicated young doctors who'd returned to their village after completing medical school. Both were intelligent men who could have established their practices anywhere in the country, but they'd chosen to take care of hometown folks.

"I'd be happy to, but I'm waiting for Leah to get back."

"No problem. We'll stop at the nurses' station and tell her where you are. Do you want a wheelchair or can you walk?"

Just that easily, it was settled. Within minutes, Taylor had left a message for Leah with the ward clerk and Gabe was heading to the man's office.

"Let's see what you have," Gabe said as he pulled a chair close enough to Taylor's desk to view the monitor.

"A formerly healthy fifty-two-year-old woman with nausea, diarrhea, vomiting, jaundice and sudden weight loss."

Gabe's instincts went on full alert. The last time he'd been in Ciuflores and helped with a clinic, he'd run into a case very similar, if not identical. At the time, he'd had limited diagnostic capabilities and had urged Hector to send the woman to a more advanced facility. "Any palpable masses?" he asked, because at the time he'd seen this particular patient he hadn't found any.

"Yes," Taylor mentioned. "In her belly."

Gabe hoped this patient wasn't the one he knew... "Labs?"

"I have the basics. There are more abnormals than not." Taylor handed Gabe a sheet of paper. "Her conjugated bilirubin is elevated, along with the liver enzymes, including alkaline phosphatase. From what I can tell, there's a lot of organ involvement."

According to the numbers, it was clear the woman had

cholestasis—a blockage in her bile duct—as well as issues with her liver. Her amylase was also off the charts and her glucose was abnormal, indicating pancreatic problems, too. As Taylor had stated, very few of her results fell within the reference range.

"They also sent a few ultrasound pictures." The older surgeon clicked a few times with his mouse and the images appeared on screen.

In spite of the grainy quality, the mass in the region of the pancreas was unmistakable and the diagnosis grim. Eighty-five percent of pancreatic masses were aggressive cancers and of those sixty to eighty percent had tumors that had spread into surrounding tissue.

"I hate to make a definitive diagnosis with so little to go on," Taylor said. "According to Dr. Aznar's email, a CT scan and MRI are out of the question."

"Hector and his colleague operate a small clinic and their resources are extremely limited. They didn't even have an ultrasound until I gave them one two months ago."

"How well do you know this Aznar fellow?"

"He's a smart fellow. Cares deeply about his patients because he grew up in the area."

"Can he handle a biopsy?"

"If he doesn't have a choice then yes, but he doesn't have any pathology capabilities. He'll have to ship the specimen to another hospital, which will take time, depending on how far it has to go." Gabe tried to remember where the nearest pathologist might be other than Mexico City, but came up blank.

"I assume they can't send their patients to a larger facility?"

"They can, but the nearest one is a half day's drive away and is only a step above their own clinic. The problem is, most of the natives either won't travel the distance or can't afford the trip, which is why internet access to specialists is so important."

Gabe leaned back in his chair. "The question is, do you think the tumor is operable?"

"It's difficult to say for sure," the nearly sixty-year-old physician said soberly. "Considering the size, one would have to guess that the cancer has already spread. The lab results seem to support that theory. If so, surgery won't help." He paused. "I assume chemotherapy isn't readily available."

"It isn't."

"Then Dr. Aznar doesn't have a choice. His patient has to go where she can receive proper testing and an accurate diagnosis. We can't discount the possibility of a benign tumor, which can be a curable condition."

"No," Gabe answered, "but even if it *is* benign, we can't guarantee a positive outcome."

He glanced at the patient ID and the name immediately jumped off the screen. Carlotta J. Salazar. His gut churned as he pictured the woman who'd come to his clinic. The same woman who lived at the local orphanage with her three precious grandchildren as the facility's main cook. From what David had told him, the poor woman hadn't had an easy life, and now a serious illness had added to her troubles. It was a good thing he would be going to Ciuflores in a couple of days. While he was there, maybe there would be something he could do for the woman who'd always fussed over his team like a grandmother.

Immediately, her three grandchildren came to mind. If he couldn't do anything for Carlotta, maybe he could do something for her family.

Taylor looked thoughtful as he stared at the images. "I like to play the odds and until we have a biopsy report, we have to. I'll email Aznar and talk him through a biopsy procedure if necessary. Meanwhile, I'll send the case on to a pancreatic specialist I know, unless you already have one in your network." He raised an eyebrow.

Gabe thought a moment. "We do. Let me call Sheldon for his contact information."

A phone call and a few clicks of a mouse later—along with

several muttered curses as Taylor clicked the wrong buttons—Taylor had an address and phone number in his inbox.

Gabe watched as Taylor painstakingly typed a short message to Hector, then another to Dr. Stephen Wilkerson, before asking Gabe's help in attaching the digital files for the specialist's review.

Finally, Taylor leaned back and grinned. "Done. Medicine has certainly changed since I first became a doctor," he said ruefully. "Who would have thought we would send images and reports around the world and back in less time than it takes to dial a phone number?"

"Who would have thought?" Gabe echoed.

"Knock, knock," Leah's voice came from the doorway. "I hear you've stolen my patient, Dr. Ewing."

Taylor rose with a hearty smile. "You heard correctly, my dear. Come in, come in. How have you been?"

"I'm great. Thanks for asking. Did you two finish your business?"

"Just now," the surgeon informed her. "I imagine you're in a hurry to get our boy home."

In Gabe's opinion, her smile seemed a bit forced, but it was a smile, nevertheless. "He is rather impatient, as you can imagine," she said.

"Then I won't keep you." He shook Gabe's hand. "Stay in touch, okay?"

"I will," Gabe promised.

In the hallway, he tried to read Leah's reaction, but couldn't. "I'll bet you were surprised to get Taylor's message," he said, to test the waters.

"Surprised to learn that you were wandering around the hospital with Taylor? A little, but, knowing how eager you were to leave, I assumed you had a good reason."

"I did. He got his first tele-medicine consult and wanted me to walk him through it."

"How did it go?"

"From a technology standpoint, great. Not so good for the

patient, though. What's really unfortunate is that I know the woman."

"Someone you've worked with?" she asked.

"Not really. Whenever my team and I visited Ciuflores, she took care of us. Cooked, did our laundry, that sort of thing."

"I'm sorry to hear she's not well. Will she recover?"

"The odds aren't in her favor." He shifted gears. "Did you get my lab results?"

"I did. Your white count is down and Jeff says you can go."

"Hot damn!" he exclaimed, pumping his fist in the air.

She grinned. "I thought you'd be pleased. As soon as we get back to the room, I'll take out your cannula and we'll be on our way."

"Fa-a-a-ntastic!"

But as they meandered through the hospital corridors to return to his starting point, he realized Leah had taken the long route. He knew she wasn't trying to give him more exercise or to delay his departure. She'd done it purely to avoid passing by the OB unit and the nursery. He'd hoped she'd gotten past her aversion, but apparently she had not.

One day, soon, they would have to clear the air about that, but not today. Today, he was finally going home.

Leah drew a bracing breath before she stepped through the garage door into the house she and Gabe had built. As she clutched the two grocery bags in her arms, a hundred memories bombarded her—memories of feeding each other strawberries during a late-night refrigerator raid to the day when she'd plunked the packet of divorce documents on the counter. She'd half expected the pages to still be there, but they were gone. Either Gabe, or Carrie Erickson, their housekeeper for the past four years, had moved them.

Asking about the folder would subtly remind him of why she'd agreed to his unholy pact, but she couldn't do it. Not only had she vowed to herself that sniping and innuendo wouldn't make the next few weeks any more bearable, but the look of sheer delight on his face as he slowly turned a three-sixty wouldn't allow her to say anything that would mar his homecoming. Cruel, she was not.

"I was afraid I'd never see this place again," he said simply. "It's good to be home."

"I'm sure it is," she answered, still trying to decide if she felt the same way. She wasn't particularly happy about being here because of all the memories, both good and bad, but Gabe had insisted she move in with him instead of vice versa. It was infuriating to realize he'd stacked the deck in his favor but, as she'd told herself many times during the last eighteen hours, this wasn't any different than enduring a mammogram. According to her mother and others who'd had one, the aggravation—and the pain—didn't last long. In the grand scheme of things, six weeks wasn't long, either.

Although perhaps once Gabe recognized and accepted that they both had fundamental differences about what they wanted in their futures, he'd sign those papers much sooner. She could only hope.

"Yeah," he said with satisfaction as he glanced through the doorway into the living room before smiling at her like a kid on Christmas morning. "Just like I remembered."

She took stock of the gleaming black granite countertops, the shiny stainless-steel appliances and the glistening cream-colored ceramic tile floor that she and Gabe had selected during what seemed a lifetime ago. A simple jar candle of her favorite Fresh Rain fragrance rested on the round table in the breakfast nook.

Nothing had changed and yet everything had.

He sniffed the air. "It even smells fresh."

"Carrie came by yesterday to air out the house and get it ready for you. For us," she corrected.

"Did you call her?" he asked.

"After our little talk. From the way the kitchen looks, she must have worked through the night dusting and polishing. She always did take good care of things."

"I'll have to call and thank her." He leaned against the counter to gaze around the room again. "If you only knew how many times I pictured this. Your fresh flowers on the table, the dishes stacked in the sink, the shoes by the door, the smell of your banana bread."

The flowers on the table had disappeared two years ago. Several months later her desire to bake had vanished and the dishes in the sink had eventually dwindled down to a coffee cup, saucer and a spoon because they'd eaten out more often than not. The only shoes by the door were the ones she'd deposited there a minute ago.

And yet could she blame him for thinking back on happier times in order to survive the most stressful period of his life?

A wrinkle appeared on his forehead, as if he realized real life wasn't comparing to his memories. "It's been a while since those days, hasn't it?"

"Yeah." Then, because she felt awkward and didn't want to say anything that might sound petty, she changed the subject. "Would you like a cup of coffee?"

"That would be great."

"Why don't you relax in the living room and I'll bring it when it's ready?"

"I'd rather sit here." He pulled a chair away from the breakfast table and sat down, wincing as he did so.

She'd noticed. "Ribs still sore?"

"Afraid so. They're better than they were, though."

"After another week or two of rest, you'll be back at the gym as usual."

"Probably," he said. "Do you still go?"

She shook her head as she poured water into the reservoir and spooned several tablespoons of Gabe's special dark roast they'd bought on their way home from the hospital. "I prefer walking or jogging outdoors." Truthfully, she'd started that so she wouldn't risk running into Gabe because he didn't work out on a set schedule.

"When I'm able to, I'd like to join you."

Surprised by his suggestion, she blurted, "But you hate to run. You always lifted weights, or swam laps."

"Nothing says I can't try something new. And I'd like to jog with you. We used to go to the park together."

"To walk," she corrected, "and it was when we were first married. That was a long time ago."

"So? Going back will be like old times. Remember when I flagged down the ice-cream truck in the middle of traffic because you wanted a vanilla cone?"

"Yes, and you almost got run over by a vehicle for it."

"True, but my quick reflexes saved the day."

"Quick reflexes?" she scoffed. "I saw that car hit your leg."

"It was a tap, not a hit," he insisted. "I didn't even get a bruise, which, if you recall, we spent hours looking for."

She remembered the evening in question quite vividly. It had been the same evening that had ended in a midnight kitchen raid for strawberries, peanut butter and chocolate ice-cream topping. The next day she'd sent their comforter to the dry cleaners to deal with the sticky stains.

"I know what you're doing," she said suddenly.

"What?"

"You're hoping to get what you want by going through the back door when you normally tear down the front."

"Is it working?" he asked hopefully.

"Not so far."

"Too bad. But for the record, I know how difficult it is for you to move into our house when you weren't mentally prepared."

His insight caught her by surprise and she simply gaped at him.

"But we have to learn to talk to each other again and dusting off the good memories seems a good place to start."

Her eyes narrowed. "Did you read a do-it-yourself marriage counseling book somewhere?"

"No. I just spent a lot of time thinking," he said simply. "So, how does my theory sound? Shall we begin there?"

She didn't want to because she sensed what would follow. She'd drop her defenses and be vulnerable, but they couldn't spend the next six weeks limiting their conversation to the weather or medicine. To be honest, she'd like to know what had been going on in Gabe's mind during those days when life had become so dark and bleak because he'd appeared so...unmoved by it all.

Or, as she'd already considered briefly, had he simply been better at hiding his reactions? Or worse yet, had she pushed him away so completely that he'd felt as if he *couldn't* talk? The latter question was one that she hadn't considered before, and the potential answer didn't sit well on her chest now. But, as he'd said, they had to start somewhere...

"Sure, why not?" she said. "We can stroll down memory lane, but I never have denied that we had some great years together. However, all good things come to an end."

"That's debatable, but for now we need to deal with a few housekeeping issues first. Moving your things comes to mind."

"I thought after you were settled, I'd run home and—"

"I'm coming with you."

She raised an eyebrow. "Afraid I won't come back?"

"No," he said solemnly. "You gave your word and I trust you. I want to come along so I can help."

"You want to *help?* You're limping worse than a Saturday night drunk, your ribs hurt if you breathe too deeply or move suddenly, and you aren't supposed to lift anything heavier than a pen."

"It's not that bad," he defended.

She cast him a you've-got-to-be-kidding look. "No offense, but let's be realistic. How much help do you think you'll be?"

"Maybe not much, but I want to go with you."

"What for? To supervise?"

"No. To keep you company."

He wanted to keep her *company?* Once again, he'd surprised her. "Oh."

"Do you mind?"

Of course she did. The little house she was renting was her childhood home—her sanctuary. She didn't want Gabe's overwhelming presence to ruin that for her.

Yet, once again, it seemed cruel to make a fuss over something so trivial, especially when they wouldn't be on the property any longer than it took to empty out her refrigerator and throw a few clothes into a travel bag.

Letting out a soft sigh, she surrendered. "Suit yourself, but if I catch you overdoing things, I'll convince Jeff to re-admit you."

"Understood. Is the coffee ready?"

She found the cups in the same cupboard where she'd always stored them and filled two. As she carried them to the table where Gabe was sitting, a brisk knock at the back door caught her off guard.

"Are you expecting someone?" she asked.

"No."

There were few people who qualified as back-door guests and she already guessed their visitor's identity. She wasn't wrong.

"Sheldon." She greeted him halfheartedly, not entirely shocked by his appearance given his eagerness to talk to Gabe while he'd been in the hospital.

Gabe's second-in-command stood on the threshold, his face somewhat apologetic. "Sorry to bother you because I know this isn't the best time, but I'd like to talk to Gabe. I promise I'll be gone before you realize I've been here."

Heaving a sigh, she stepped aside wordlessly and tried not to read anything into the way Gabe's eyes brightened at the sight of the familiar face.

"What's up, Shel?" he asked.

"The memorial service for Will and Ramon is set for day after tomorrow," he said.

"You worked fast."

"The families wanted it this way," he said simply.

Gabe simply nodded. "Of course."

"And," Sheldon continued, "we've been trying to make head or tail out of your notes for our Ecuador project and haven't had any luck. We're scheduled to go there in two weeks, and to make matters worse the health ministry is dragging its feet over the permits again. Would you mind setting me on the right track?"

"Not a problem," Gabe answered.

"Wait a minute," she protested. "You just got home from the hospital. You're supposed to *rest*, not work."

"This isn't physical labor," Gabe pointed out. "I'm only answering a few questions."

"That's right," Sheldon chimed in. "As soon as Gabe brings me up to speed and we sort through the problems, I'll be out of here. Ten minutes, tops."

"Do *any* of your projects run smoothly?" she countered.

"Lots do, but not this one. While you're waiting, why don't you relax? Shoot, lie down for a few minutes. I know you didn't sleep much last night."

He wanted her to *lie down*? When she had so much to do, the least of which was changing her address? Wasn't it enough that he'd blackmailed her into spending the coming weeks together, simply because it was what *he* wanted? Disbelief instantly filled her.

"It's only for a few minutes," Gabe coaxed. "Sheldon wouldn't be here unless it was important."

And therein lay the rub. His work *was* important. She knew so many people who wouldn't have gotten the medical help they'd needed now did, and it was all because of Gabe. The problem was with her. She simply wasn't as philanthropic of his time as he was. Perhaps she needed to live in a third world country to get her husband's attention.

Deciding she was being petty, she sighed. "You're right. Everything else can wait."

His gaze searched hers and, apparently satisfied by the acceptance he saw, he cupped the side of her face. "I know this isn't working out the way we'd planned."

"It isn't the first time."

"I promise we'll hurry."

"Yeah," Sheldon interjected. "I only need a few minutes."

Leah had learned long ago that "a few minutes" was code for "a few hours", if not longer. So much for things being different…

On the other hand, Sheldon probably did have a lot of questions. Gabe was involved in every aspect of the foundation and unless he'd left copious notes—which he wasn't known to do because he carried so much of his information in his head—Sheldon had been left to unravel the mess left behind.

Resigned to the inevitable, she simply nodded before she addressed Sheldon. "Would you like a cup of coffee while you're working?"

"I'd love one," he said fervently.

As soon as she handed a fresh mug to Sheldon, Gabe stepped forward to brush a kiss on her cheek. Instant awareness shot through her as she felt his lips touch her skin and she inhaled the scent that was only Gabe. *Stop that*, she mentally chided her traitorous body.

"Thanks," he murmured. "Would you like to join us?"

Another first. Well, not really a first. At one time he'd included her when he'd discussed foundation business at home, but that had ended after their adoption had fallen through. Then he'd stopped asking, as if he couldn't bear to be around her any more than necessary.

"Maybe next time," she answered. "While I'm waiting, I'll make my lists."

"Good idea." He turned away, then stopped short. "Is my computer still here?"

"It should be. I haven't taken anything," Leah replied. In fact, she'd been postponing the task of cleaning out the house to list it with a real estate agent. Now, she was grateful she'd dragged her feet. It would have been awful for Gabe to suddenly find himself homeless. "Sheldon?"

He shrugged. "I haven't taken anything, either."

Gabe seemed relieved by the news, which was understandable. "I presume you didn't cut off my network access or delete my files?"

Sheldon grinned. "Do I look stupid, boss? Of course not."

As the two men headed toward Gabe's home office, Leah was certain they'd both lose track of time once they began discussing work.

She found a pencil and notepad in the drawer near the telephone and sat down to begin her list. Unfortunately, her mind couldn't get past the fact that they hadn't been in the house for five minutes and she was already competing with his job. Her temper simmered.

She wanted to march in and yell at him, to remind him of his "things will be different" speech, but doing so with Sheldon in the room would only make the situation uncomfortable for everyone. But if Gabe wanted complete and total honesty, she intended to give it to him. No more holding things inside, no more being the sweet, forgiving, *pushover* wife.

Yet as she stared blindly through the window into the garden she'd once loved, her irritation faded. She hated the way she'd overreacted, even though no one knew it except her. Sheldon wasn't purposely sabotaging their life. Deadlines had to be met and questions had to be answered so the job could go forward, but what would he have done if Gabe hadn't been here? He would have muddled through on his own and probably done a wonderful job.

On the other hand, did Gabe have to run every time Sheldon, or anyone else at his office, called? She had so many questions and so few answers, which, according to Gabe, was what the next few weeks was all about.

Six weeks suddenly seemed to stretch into forever.

Gabe had tried to watch the time—he really had. However, one thing had led to another and by the time he'd checked the clock, two hours had passed.

So much for his "few minutes" promise, he thought glumly. "Sorry, Shel, but that's it for today."

Sheldon glanced at his watch and cursed under his breath. "Hey, man, I'm so sorry. It's just been such a relief having you back that the questions just kept coming."

"I understand."

"Tell Leah I'm sorry, too, and that I'll make it up to her."

"I'll tell her," he said, before Sheldon let himself out. Unfortunately, he had more to tell her than Sheldon's promise of restitution. A sincere apology was in order. He'd vowed things would be different but so far he'd failed his first challenge. Now he had to hope she'd give him another chance, although he would wager his old Beamer that she'd simply been waiting for him to screw up so she could say "I told you so" before she walked out the door. She'd given him one pass already in the hospital when she'd questioned him about his nightmares. He didn't think she'd do it again.

Yet he wasn't willing to surrender so soon. If that was her plan, then he'd argue they were both bound to make mistakes on their way to getting things right.

Practicing his apology, he slowly made his way past the living room to the kitchen, but she wasn't there. Thinking she'd gone upstairs and taken a nap, as he'd suggested, he ignored the pain in his leg and grimly climbed the stairs, hoping to find her in their bedroom, tucked under the covers, fast asleep.

At least, he hoped she was there because *he* wanted to wake her and he knew exactly how he wanted to do it. He'd first run a light finger along the side of her face before moving down her neck to take a detour along her collarbone. From there, he'd meander through a most luscious valley until she finally reached for him.

Anticipation, coupled with his months of celibacy, created a physical response so strong he could hardly turn the doorknob. When he did, he saw the master bedroom's king-size bed covered in the familiar green-and-gold comforter she'd bought when she'd decorated the room. A variety of matching pillows were artfully arranged near the headboard, but the bed itself was empty.

Leah wasn't there.

He checked every room upstairs—the guest room and even the nursery—but she wasn't in any of them.

He went downstairs, through the house and into the back-yard where she'd once loved to sit and enjoy the butterfly garden.

No Leah.

Where had she gone? More importantly, was she coming back? His gut churned at the possibility.

No, he decided logically, she would be back. She wanted his signature too much to give up so quickly. She was prob-ably running an errand or, having grown tired of waiting for him, she'd left for her place without him. No doubt she was on her way back this very moment.

Reassured by that thought, he returned to his office—his favorite room of the house. They'd spent many comfortable hours within these four walls, he realized as he sat behind the oak desk Leah had given him one Christmas. Leah would often curl up in the overstuffed chair with one of her fiction books while he'd read through his stack of medical publi-cations or taken care of business paperwork. Music or the television would play in the background and when they had both tired of whatever it was they'd been doing, they'd put the smooth desk surface to good use.

Now, though, instead of being cluttered with medical and cooking magazines or her latest knitting pattern, the highly polished wood only held his pen and pencil set, a framed photo of the two of them, which had been taken shortly after she'd learned she was pregnant, and a desk calendar with its top page showing the day he'd left on his last trip.

He didn't need to open the top left-hand drawer to know what it contained. A phone book, the *Yellow Pages*, and the divorce papers she'd delivered. With any luck at all, those doc-uments would soon be shredded and residing in the trash.

He glanced at the wall clock and saw another hour had passed. Telling himself not to worry about things like car accidents, ambulances or the county morgue, he broke down and dialed her cell phone number from memory, but his call went straight to her voice mail.

He told himself to wait. Traffic could have snarled, checkout lines could have been horrific, or she'd simply got caught up browsing and had forgotten to watch the time. He hoped the latter was the case because then he wouldn't feel so badly about doing the same.

After another fifteen minutes he simply couldn't wait any longer. He had to do *something*, even if he had to drive from one end of the city to the other, but he'd find her.

One way or another, he *would*.

CHAPTER SIX

LEAH watched the play of Gabe's muscles underneath his cotton shirt as he soaped her little blue Mustang. It was still almost hard to believe he'd married her when he could have had his pick of all the beautiful women in the world, but the shiny new ring on her finger said it was true. So did their marriage license and the wedding picture proofs she'd picked up from the photographer that morning.

Suddenly, a blast of cold water struck her chest.

"Gabe," she protested. "Look what you've done. I'm all wet."

His appreciative glance suddenly wiped away her irritation.

"So am I," he reminded her.

"But I wanted to wear this to my parents' house," she protested without heat. "Now I'll have to change."

"Can I help?" he asked hopefully.

"You can't." She pretended to pout as she struck up a sultry pose. "You're busy."

"Not anymore," he said, immediately shutting off the tap.

In a flash, she was in their bedroom, entwined in the sheets as his mouth and hands roamed over her body. "Oh, Gabe," she murmured as he caressed her breast and nipped at her neck. "That feels…"

"Wonderful?"

"Yes."

"How about this?" His fingers skittered a path down her body to a secret spot only he had found.

She arched in his arms. "Oh, my..."

Suddenly, the pleasant, swirling sensation disappeared as she felt something solid underneath her.

That wasn't right. How had the mattress become that hard...and bony?

She wiggled, wanting Gabe to fly her back to the clouds before she'd been so strangely and rudely interrupted, but she couldn't get comfortable. She and Gabe had fit so well together, but now there was this thing between them.

She elbowed the object, but it wouldn't budge. Irritated now, she pushed harder, but it only moved a fraction. Determined to remove this strange obstacle, she raised herself on one elbow and opened her eyes to see just what had dared to ruin her romantic interlude—

Leah gasped as she realized Gabe was lying beside her. Lying in *her* bed, in *her* house, on top of *her* quilt. And right now he was watching her with his intensely dark eyes.

This is certainly awkward. "What...?" She swallowed. "What are you doing here?" she asked faintly.

"Looking for you."

Oh, dear. "Is everything all right?"

His gaze didn't waver. "You tell me."

Instinctively, she understood his unspoken question. "I'm not upset because Sheldon came by," she assured him. "Well, I was at first, but I got over it once I put myself in his shoes."

The intensity in his eyes faded and he visibly relaxed. "I'm glad."

"By the way, what time is it?"

"Quarter before five."

She sank onto her back and flung her arm over her eyes. If he was right, then she'd been here for over four hours, and had been sleeping for most of them.

"How...how did you get in?" she asked.

"I recognized your fake rock in the flower bed near the

front door. You really should find out a better place to hide your house key," he said.

"Apparently so, if all sorts of riff-raff can find it," she said meaningfully.

He laughed at her veiled barb. "Let this be a lesson to you."

"How long have you been here?" she asked.

"About an hour."

An hour? "You should have woken me."

"I could have, but you were tired."

She had been. She'd slept very little the previous night, watching over Gabe and helping him through his nightmares. Tired or not, though, she hadn't planned her afternoon to turn out this way, and she told him so.

"Oh?" he asked, more curious than skeptical.

"After you didn't show any signs of wrapping up your conversation with Sheldon, I decided to run here, pack my things and get back before you noticed I was gone." She offered a weak grin. "Obviously, my plans didn't turn out the way I'd hoped."

"I'll admit we took longer than I'd intended," he admitted, "but when Sheldon went home and you weren't in the house, I started to wonder..."

"I should have left a note," she said, "but, honestly, this was supposed to be a simple, thirty-minute errand. When I walked into the house, though, a shower sounded good, and then the bed looked so comfortable. I decided to lie down for a few minutes and, well, the next thing I know, you're here in bed with me."

She narrowed her eyes, but before she could question him he put on a complete air of innocence. "You told me I should rest, so I did."

"I didn't mean you should do it in *my* bed."

"It isn't as if we made love while you were dead to the world," he calmly pointed out. "Furthermore, we aren't breaking any moral or legal laws if we share the same mattress. If it makes you feel better, notice how I'm on top of the blanket and you're not."

She clutched the sheet to her chest, aware that only a flimsy piece of fabric was between them. Granted, he wouldn't see anything he hadn't seen before, but it was the principle of the matter. They were a hairbreadth away from a divorce, for heaven's sake!

"Just so you know—we may be sharing a house, but that's *all* we're sharing. I'm taking the guest bedroom."

"We're trying to make our marriage work, Leah," he reminded her. "As I recall, our bedroom was the one place we didn't have any problems."

"I don't deny how wonderful our sex life was, but making love now only clouds our issues."

He looked somewhat disgruntled, although not surprised. "I was afraid you'd say that," he said ruefully.

"Because you know I'm right."

"Okay," he agreed. "I'll accept your decision. "For now.""

Which meant he would address this subject again, but at this moment he was backing off. She would be satisfied with that, although if Gabe ever got a glimmer of her dream, he'd do his best to change her mind. Quickly.

"Did I…?" She paused. "Say or do…anything?"

He grinned. "You mean, like crawl all over me and whisper sweet nothings in my ear?"

Oh, dear. "Did I?" she asked, bracing herself for the worst.

"All I can say is that your elbow should be registered as a lethal weapon." He rubbed his side.

She was too horrified by the possibility of having caused him serious damage to be embarrassed, and she began pulling at his shirt to look for evidence. "Did I hurt you? Oh, my, your *ribs*!" she wailed.

He caught her hand. "They're fine," he said. "You didn't hurt me. Well, maybe a little, but hearing you say my name was worth the pain."

She was mortified. She'd never convince him she wanted

him out of her life if he'd heard her moan his name or if he knew he'd starred in her erotic dream.

"So," he said matter-of-factly, "do we want to stay in bed or get up and gather your things?"

"Get up," she said promptly.

"Okay. Ladies first."

She raised her eyebrow. "Not a chance, buster. As you well know, I'm only wearing this sheet and I'm not dropping it. I'll see you downstairs."

"Spoilsport."

He gingerly swung one leg over the edge and rolled upright with a small grunt, reminding Leah of his injuries. "I assume you haven't packed anything yet?"

She was embarrassed to answer. "No."

"Then I'll put on a pot of coffee." With that, he limped from the room.

For a minute Leah simply lay there, realizing how her best-laid plan had gone awry. Gabe's presence had already tainted her safe haven, much as the spirits of the two children she'd considered hers had tainted the house she and Gabe had built. There, she'd done her best to confine the atmosphere by locking the door to the nursery, but the gloom had invaded the rest of the house like a noxious fume and nothing she did could dispel it. The only way she could break free had been to move where she didn't see memories everywhere she turned.

Now, thanks to not setting an alarm, to not returning before he'd realized she'd left, she wouldn't ever banish the image of him in this specific bedroom and in this specific bed.

Damage control was in order, which meant she had to get him out of there as quickly as she could. She dashed to the bathroom and shimmied into a fresh pair of jeans and a clean T-shirt.

Next, she pulled her suitcases out of the closet and began tossing in clothes haphazardly. A quick sweep of the bathroom's counter and medicine cabinet took care of her personal items and within minutes she was packed. Neatness, in this instance, didn't count.

Downstairs, she set her cases by the door. Through the window, she caught a glimpse of Gabe's SUV parked at the curb.

"Your vehicle's outside," she said inanely as she accepted the mug Gabe handed her.

"How else was I supposed to get here?" he asked.

"Sheldon didn't give you a ride?" she asked.

"No."

"You *drove*? Are you *crazy*?"

He snagged a butterscotch out of the candy bowl on the nearby end table and nonchalantly unwrapped it. "I may have been out of the country for a few weeks, but I still have my driver's license."

"This isn't about the legality. It's about your health," she scolded. "You shouldn't be behind the wheel with your bum leg and sore ribs. Your reflexes are compromised and what if you're in an accident? You could be seriously injured, even killed! Not to mention the damage an air bag could do."

"Those scenarios are possible," he said, clearly unconcerned at the prospect, "but after surviving a plane crash, a car wreck seems mild in comparison."

"For heaven's sake, Gabe. You were lucky once, but you aren't invincible."

He folded the wrapper in half then in half again, as if he had nothing else to concern him, but she knew his casual air belied his sharp-eyed gaze and keen powers of observation. "You seem worried over something that didn't and probably wouldn't happen."

She couldn't believe he was asking her that question. "Why wouldn't I worry when you do something foolish?"

He shrugged. "It's nice to know you care."

"Of course I care," she snapped. "You're my—" She stopped short, unable to supply the word he was obviously waiting to hear and feeling as if he'd led her down this path.

"Husband?" he supplied helpfully.

She raised her chin. "Yes. For now."

"Then, as your husband, don't you think I'd worry about you, too?"

"I already explained and apologized for not leaving a note," she pointed out. "If I'd known I was so tired, I would have taken a nap when you suggested it."

"But you thought you could get by without one."

She nodded as she sipped her coffee, pleasantly surprised he'd remembered her preference for peppermint creamer and two packets of non-calorie sweetener. "That and...." She debated explaining the rest, but he wanted honesty, so she'd give it to him. "It just seemed as if once again you were telling me what to do."

"I'm sorry you thought so because I was only offering a suggestion," he said slowly. "It seemed kinder to suggest a nap than to mention the bags under your eyes or your haggard appearance."

No doubt she *had* looked like death warmed over—a twenty-four-hour stint in the hospital tended to do that to a person. "You're right, it was," she admitted. "I was cranky and finding fault. I'll try not to be so sensitive next time."

"And I'll keep Sheldon's interruptions to a minimum."

"Do you really think it's possible?"

He grinned. "You bet, especially if I don't answer the phone or the door."

"So you'll let the phone screen your calls and I get to weed out your visitors."

"Precisely."

"The next question is, will *you* be able to stay away from the office?" she asked, thinking of the hours he'd devoted to his foundation. Twelve- to sixteen-hour days hadn't been uncommon during their last year together. "I know how difficult it is for you to relinquish the driver's seat of your organization."

"I can, and I will," he said. "During our time in the jungle, Jack and I speculated on what might be happening here at home without me, and neither of us saw a pretty picture. My father wouldn't have agreed with me, but it isn't good for the entire workings of the foundation to hinge on one person. Until I implement more permanent changes, Sheldon is in charge. After I take hold of the reins again, I plan to delegate more."

"I'm sure you'd like to implement your ideas, but I'm not convinced life will be any different than it was before."

"I haven't convinced you *yet*," he corrected. "But I will. In fact, I'm willing to dissolve the trust fund and turn the foundation over to someone else if time becomes an issue."

His news clearly caught her off guard because she stared at him with the same incredulity he'd seen on her face when the ambulance doors had opened. "You're kidding."

"I'm not."

"I can't believe you're offering to relinquish your family's legacy. You've helped so many people—"

"I learned what's important in life," he said simply. "Yes, the foundation fills a need for a lot of people, but in the end my wife has to come first."

"Why?" she blurted out. "I know you cut back on your hours when we thought we were starting our family, but our situation is different now."

"Not really," he mentioned. "We're still a couple and I want to spend time with you."

He made it sound as if their future was settled, but in her eyes it still wasn't. And yet, if they were to have any *hope* of a future, they certainly had to do more than see each other in passing.

However, being around each other twenty-four seven meant that certain subjects were bound to come up. Certain subjects on which she'd already made her stand. Certain subjects that had brought them to the brink of a divorce…

She studied him through narrowed eyes. "And what happens if, by some miracle, we restore our relationship? What then? What's next on your agenda?"

He frowned. "I don't have an agenda, other than avoiding the divorce court."

"It isn't in the back of your mind to convince me to try the adoption route again? If that's your end game, then we may as well visit my attorney now rather than later."

"That isn't my plan," he insisted. "Whether we have children or not, we can still have a wonderful marriage. Just the two of us."

He sounded sincere and nothing in his eyes hinted at subterfuge, but she knew how badly he'd wanted children and she said so.

"Yes, I wanted to raise a couple of kids and still do if the opportunity arises," he admitted, "but our relationship comes first. If that isn't healthy, there's nothing left."

His quick response and his calm gaze caught her off guard. She hadn't expected him to give up his heart's desire so easily and it startled her to the point where she couldn't find the words to reply.

"Is that why you've been digging in your heels about this divorce business?" he asked, clearly amazed. "You're trying to save me from myself, aren't you?"

"It isn't fair to ask you to give up something you've desperately wanted and dreamed of," she defended. "You'll wake up one morning and realize you've wasted all those years and then we'll be back in the same boat, sailing down the same river to nowhere. I can't go through that again—"

"Will you let me be the judge of what I want?"

"Children are all you've ever talked about. As an only child, you wanted a houseful, you said."

"I did, because I believe siblings teach life lessons that an only child doesn't learn. Things like sharing everything from toys to parental attention and getting along with others, even when they irritate the heck out of us. But, Leah, we have to play the cards we're dealt and if we don't have children, then so be it."

"Then why…?" She bit her lip in indecision.

"Why what?"

"Why did you push so hard for us to adopt right after we

lost Andrew? You'd lost your chance to be a father and you grabbed at the first opportunity that came along."

"Is that what you think?" he asked, incredulous. "That I rushed into the adoption only because I wanted to be a *father*?"

"Didn't you?"

"No," he exploded. "Absolutely, not! I did it for *you*."

"How was your decision for me, Gabe? I was still grieving for my baby and any future children, and the next thing I knew we're trying to complete home studies and prepare for another baby."

He raked his hair with his fingers. "Hindsight says we should have waited, but at the time the opportunity seemed heaven sent. It would have been, too, but no one anticipated Whitney changing her mind in the final hour."

Leah let out a sigh. No, no one had known or even guessed the outcome would turn out completely different than everyone had planned. Whitney Ellis, the birth mother, had been so sure of her decision—until the time came for her to live with it.

"I had to do *something*, Leah, because I was losing you. You wouldn't talk. You wouldn't tell me how you felt. Later, after we began discussing adoption and you met Whitney, you came around. You were happy again."

After she'd recovered from her initial surprise and the situation had felt real and not just a dream, she had been. Deliriously happy.

"Then," he continued, "as soon as she decided to keep her baby, everything fell apart again. And then, before I knew it, you were moving out."

Gabe had struggled with so many conflicting emotions during those long months, but the day she'd packed her bags had been the bleakest day of his life. The day she'd asked for a divorce hadn't been a high point of his thirty-eight years, either. However, this was the first time he realized she had attributed selfish motives to him.

Then again, how could he have guessed? They'd never expressed themselves this openly before.

He should have pushed her harder to unburden herself in the weeks and months after their adoption had fallen through. He'd waited for her to broach the subject, thinking she'd talk when she was ready, but she never had. On the other hand, he'd *wanted* to talk, to pour out his disappointment and his pain, but he hadn't known how or where to begin. Consequently, they'd never discussed what had obviously lain so heavily on their hearts until eventually they'd found solace in other ways. He'd taken refuge in his work and she'd accepted a relief position at the hospital.

In the end, they'd drifted apart. Now he was trying to steer them back together, unable to believe he might be too late.

"Regardless of what you were trying to do, I don't want to live through the same experience," she said in a flat tone. "Putting our lives on display to birth parents in the hope they'll choose us, being interviewed and trying not to sound over-eager, not to mention the waiting, the *interminable* waiting. Then, after all that, our hopes and plans can fall through at a moment's notice."

"I understand how you feel."

"Do you, Gabe?"

"I went through the same disappointments you did," he pointed out. "It wasn't easy for me, either."

She frowned and cocked her head to study him. "You didn't act upset."

"I was. I wouldn't let myself show it because I felt like I had to be strong for you."

"I see." She paused. "Now that you know how I feel, if we reconcile—and that's a big *if*—would you be satisfied with my decision?"

"Absolutely," he said firmly, "As long as you don't let fear influence your choice. But whatever we do, whichever route we take, we have to move forward. Doing what we've done before—avoiding the issue, locking off a room of our house— didn't work then and it won't work now.

"That said," he continued, "at this particular point in time we have to concentrate on *us*. When we're on track again, the rest of our concerns about families and homes and jobs will fall into place."

Her expression suggested that she was skeptical, but if she truly thought he'd only been trying to fill *his* emotional needs, then he simply had to prove to her how wrong she'd been. Their future wouldn't be secure until she trusted him to mean what he'd just said.

"You can say those other things don't matter, but they've influenced our marriage."

"Then we'll deal with those things as they come up. What do you say, Leah? I know you aren't a quitter."

She sighed. "I don't have a choice. I have to play your game."

Obviously, she still felt as if she was being blackmailed— that she simply had to endure all this unpleasantness so she could get what she wanted. And yet, after lying beside her on the bed, hearing her whisper his name in her sleep, he suspected she still harbored feelings for him. He simply needed to tap into those.

"Yes," he said bluntly. "For the next six weeks, anyway."

She nodded, plainly resigned to their agreement.

Then, because he didn't know what else to say, he gestured around the room. "How much of this shall we take with us?"

"Just the afghan and my knitting bag." She pointed to a corner where yarn spilled out of a canvas tote. "If I need anything else, I can always get it later. Meanwhile, the refrigerator comes next."

He followed her into the kitchen, noticing Leah's touch wherever he looked. Silk sunflowers and wheat stalks sprouted out of several slender vases and lined the top of the kitchen cabinets. The ceramic bowl they'd bought at a flea market held fruit in the middle of the table. Her purse lay on the counter, her billfold and keys spilling out of the open flap. And several pairs of shoes stood in a neat row by the back door.

This was how a house should be, he thought. It should look lived in, not sterile and lifeless, like his. In a few short hours their house would look like he remembered, filled with color and flowers and the organized clutter that had always seemed to follow Leah. He could hardly wait.

"What made you decide to move into your parents' house?" he asked. "I thought they were going to sell it when they moved to Oklahoma to be near your sister."

To spoil their grandchildren, Tricia Jordan, Leah's mother, had told him. Although Leah hadn't seemed to begrudge them their decision, it had to be difficult for her to know that her sister was as fertile as a bunny while Leah's branch of the family tree had withered.

"They'd intended to," she admitted, "but the Realtor suggested they'd get a much better price if they updated it. So, when I wanted a place of my own, I moved in with the understanding I'd redecorate and modernize."

He glanced around the room. "You did a wonderful job. You always did have a good eye for detail."

"Thanks."

"Can you show me the rest?"

He saw her hesitation—as if she didn't want to share this with him—before she finally shrugged. "Sure, why not?"

Gabe followed her through the dining room, back to the living room, then upstairs to the three bedrooms and a bathroom. The walls had all been freshly painted in neutral colors and airy curtains covered the windows.

"Quite an ambitious undertaking to work on by yourself," he remarked as they returned to the kitchen.

"I didn't mind. I needed to keep busy."

"I suppose." He noticed a collage of photos on the refrigerator and strolled over for a closer look. The pictures were all scenes he remembered, but one in particular stood out.

"I'd forgotten all about this," he said offhandedly as he pointed to the snapshot of the two of them at a summer carnival, posing in front of the duck-shoot booth. "I spent a small fortune trying to win this giraffe."

She came close to peer around his shoulder and smiled. "You were determined to win that prize. I think it cost you more than the animal was worth, though."

"Yeah, but we wouldn't have had nearly as much fun."

"Probably not," she agreed. "You were bound and determined to hit the grand prize duck."

The concept had been simple—to shoot the toy ducks floating past with a suction-cup dart gun. Knocking over specially marked ducks earned special prizes and he'd decided early on which one he'd wanted.

He grinned. "It took me, what—an hour? As I recall, you named it Gemma. Because of the purple jewel around her neck."

The jewel was actually a piece of colored plastic, but it was pretty and sure to catch a baby's eye, which was why Leah had insisted the giraffe would be the perfect addition to their nursery. Now the toy stood behind a closed door, gathering dust instead of occupying a child's attention.

An image of the nursery they'd designed flashed his mind's eye, accompanied by the scent of baby powder and the tinkling music of a crib mobile.

"Would it be easier if we started over in a new house?" he asked. "A clean slate, so to speak?"

"You're getting ahead of yourself again," she pointed out. "We don't even know if we can make a go of our relationship and you're already talking about new homes?"

She clearly still hadn't bought into the notion they could make their marriage work, but he refused to consider otherwise.

"I know everything between us is unsettled, but we have to approach our relationship as if it can and will succeed. If you recall, we both agreed we'd give this our full commitment, and that means we can't entertain thoughts of failure.

"Besides," he continued, "I'm not suggesting we sell our house and buy a new one next week. My idea is simply something to think about, especially when we both know there's one room you can't bear to enter."

"Going into the nursery isn't easy," she admitted, "but even if our life together was settled, I'm not certain a new house is the answer, especially if you spend the majority of your time either at the office or jetting around the world. Any marriage where one party is thousands of miles and three time zones away three weeks out of every four is going to suffer under the strain. Call me selfish, but I don't want to be philanthropic with your time."

"Like I said, Jack and Sheldon will be taking a more active role in the foundation," he assured her.

Wearing a puzzled wrinkle on her forehead, she met his gaze. "This sounds crazy, but I feel as if an imposter has replaced my real husband."

He smiled. "No imposter. I'm the real guy."

She paced a few steps before she faced him. "I appreciate your offer of a different house," she finally said, "but let's follow your advice to focus on us and deal with permanent living arrangements later."

"Fair enough," he said, satisfied with his first real sign of progress.

CHAPTER SEVEN

AFTER dinner that evening, Gabe pushed his empty plate aside and leaned back in his chair. "That was delicious, Leah. You always were a wonderful cook."

His praise brought a heated blush to Leah's face. "It was only scrambled eggs and toast," she chided. "Hardly an impressive meal."

"Maybe not to you, but it was to me. 'Impressive' is a matter of perspective."

"I suppose," she said, unconvinced by his assurance but grateful for his appreciation, "but I should have fixed something more substantial, like the chicken breast or the sirloin steak we bought this afternoon."

"Or we could have gone out for dinner, as I suggested," he said.

After hurriedly packing her necessities and driving them across town in their vehicles, she'd wanted to organize the kitchen and her closet before calling an end to the day. Visiting a restaurant would have taken far more of her evening than she'd wanted to spare.

Plus, she'd have been Gabe's captive audience while their meal was being prepared. She wasn't ready for that, yet. It was one thing to have a civil conversation in the privacy of their home. It was another to hold a conversation where they would be under public scrutiny.

"It would have taken longer to get ready than it did to scramble a few eggs," she remarked, "and chances were we would have run into someone we knew who would have wanted to visit. I still have a lot I'd like to accomplish tonight."

The real problem, in her eyes, had been the possibility of well-meaning friends congratulating them on being a couple again. She certainly didn't want to navigate that particular minefield.

"Whatever the reason, I appreciate the trouble you went to. Simple meal or not, what I had was perfect," he declared. "After all, just this morning you said I needed to go easy on my stomach."

"It seems like we had that conversation ages ago."

"Considering how hard you worked this afternoon, I'm not surprised," he said. "Where you found the energy to accomplish what we did, I'll never know."

"I didn't do that much," she said.

Gabe had wanted to empty her house, lock, stock and barrel, but she hadn't been ready to go that far. Fortunately, she'd been able to use the excuse of minimal storage and Gabe's sore ribs to dissuade him. However, she sensed he would have ignored his sore ribs to haul whatever she wanted, regardless of how big, bulky or heavy it was.

"We could have accomplished more if you'd let me," he complained good-naturedly.

"You heard the doctor's orders. No lifting."

"And I obeyed," he answered.

"Then why did I end up scolding you for carrying boxes you shouldn't?"

Remembering how she'd huffed whenever she'd caught him, then pull the load out of his arms, brought a smile to Gabe's face. At first, he'd been affronted by how little she'd allowed him to carry. Then it had become a game to see how much he could get away with. Best of all, being caught and hearing her scold only meant that she cared, even if she wasn't ready to admit it…

To his great relief, though, most of her things were back at home where they belonged, the refrigerator and pantry had been restocked, and the house that had previously looked like a model home now had a lived-in appearance.

He couldn't be happier.

Well, he could be, he amended, if Leah had moved into the master suite instead of the guest room, but being under the same roof was better than the alternative and with luck the hall would only separate them for a short time. Meanwhile, his vision of Leah tucking her finger under his collar and leading him upstairs would give him something to dream about and work toward...

"More coffee?" she asked as she rose to grab his mug.

"I've had enough caffeine for one day. I won't sleep tonight as it is." At her questioning glance, he added, "Too excited about being home, I guess."

"It doesn't quite seem real yet, does it?" she asked softly.

"No. I'm half-afraid I'll wake up and find myself still in the jungle," he confessed.

"I've been thinking along the same lines—that I'll discover your return was nothing more than wishful thinking."

He nodded, grateful she understood his fears so clearly. He only hoped she didn't press for details about the crash or the events afterwards. Yes, he'd answer because being open and honest was part of their agreement, but he'd really rather not revisit such a traumatic episode when he wanted to revel in her company on their first night together.

"I'm sure the truth will soak in soon enough," he said casually. "I certainly wouldn't be able to ignore the facts if you warmed your cold toes against my leg. How your feet can be such icicles, I'll never know."

Her answering chuckle was a melody he hadn't heard for a long while. He wasn't particularly surprised by how rusty it sounded—she'd had little to laugh about during the past few years. As for the smile she gave him...it was the sort that brightened a man's day no matter how difficult or ugly it had been, and reminded him of the girl in the carnival photo. The joyful woman with whom he'd fallen in love hadn't disappeared—she'd only been hiding behind a dark cloud.

Restoring their formerly close relationship suddenly seemed elementary. The key to rekindling their marriage was to rekindle Leah's spark, he decided, and he was just the man to do it.

"It's a gift," she said virtuously. "Although I recall offering to wear socks."

"My way of warming up your feet was more fun." He wriggled his eyebrows.

Once again, her face turned a familiar rosy hue. "It was," she agreed. "Good thing it's summer and cold feet aren't a problem. Shall we clear the dishes? I'm ready to relax for a while."

As she jumped up, he also rose. "Relaxing on the deck sounds good," he said, carrying his own place setting to the sink. "But do you know the best part about dinner tonight?"

"So few dishes?"

"Hardly. It reminded me of old times."

Her hands froze over the faucet and she stared at him as if he'd sprouted an extra nose. "Old times?"

"Yeah. Remember when we were first married? I'd come home from the hospital, starving to death but too exhausted to stay awake, and you'd fix this very meal for me so I could eat before I fell asleep on my feet."

She smiled, her tentative expression disappearing again. "And sometimes you did. I always said I should publish a cookbook—*101 Scrambled Egg Recipes*."

"Or created your own show on the Food Network."

This time she laughed, a full-bodied laugh that sounded like the carefree Leah she'd once been. The same Leah who'd found happiness in small things like sunsets, the neighbor girl's kitten, and the wildflower he'd pilfered from Mrs. O'Shea's garden near their garage before he'd walked in the door. The same Leah who hadn't been able to wait for their love to grow into a family.

"It wouldn't have been on the air long," she said lightly as she shut off the faucet and slid their plates into the soapy water. "Frankly, I was getting to the point where I thought I'd sprout feathers if I swallowed another egg, scrambled or otherwise. I shudder to think what our cholesterol levels were."

"Ah, but back then I didn't care. I was more interested in sleep, food, and…" he snaked an arm around her waist, pulled her close and planted a swift kiss against her mouth "…my wife, although not necessarily in that order."

Her small intake of breath proved that she definitely wasn't immune to his touch. "What are you doing?" she asked.

"What I should have done a long time ago," he told her. "I'm focusing on us."

Leah knew that for the next six weeks to be bearable, they had to find their footing when dealing with each other. Over the next two days they talked and they laughed, but controversial subjects were avoided, although she didn't know if that was by chance or design. Oddly enough, she found herself feeling…content.

She told herself it was only because she was within weeks of settling her life once and for all. She'd obtain Gabe's signature and that would be that. Her feelings had nothing to do with discovering how she could enjoy his company.

However well their temporary truce was holding, the door at the top of the stairs remained locked. She would have to venture inside to face her ghosts before long because her grace period would eventually run out, but in the meantime she'd lump that ugly bit of their past in with what he'd called "the rest of the stuff".

The only tense moments came when Leah followed Gabe into their house after the memorial service for his colleagues. Although he seemed to be bearing up well, she recognized the strain he'd been hiding underneath the smiles he'd shown to everyone.

"Would you like some coffee?"

He jerked at his Windsor knot as he headed into his office. "I've had enough caffeine, thanks."

She trailed after him. "A glass of wine?"

"No."

"Something to eat? I noticed you didn't sample any of the snacks after the ceremony."

"I don't want anything."

His clipped tone spoke volumes about his mood, but Leah knew how destructive brooding was. How ironic to find herself in circumstances where their former roles were reversed. This time *he* was the one hurting and *she* was the one who wanted to banish the pain but couldn't find the key to doing so.

"Okay," she said with equanimity as he sank into his executive chair. "When you are, let me know." She perched on the desk's edge. "You delivered a beautiful eulogy today. I know how difficult it was to share your personal stories and anecdotes."

"Their families deserved to hear them."

"You did an excellent job. I didn't know Will and Ramon as well as you did, but from the few times I'd been around them, I could tell you'd described their personalities and characters perfectly."

"They were good men."

"Theresa was especially grateful for your kind words. She said she has more wonderful things to tell her baby when he grows up." She paused. "I didn't know she was pregnant."

"She just found out. Ramon never knew."

"I'm sure he does now," she said softly.

He made a noise that could have meant anything from agreement to skepticism. "What did you feel when she told you?" he asked.

She thought for a moment. "Surprise. Sadness that she'd have to raise the baby alone and that Ramon would never enjoy being a father. Happiness that she'd have someone to remember him by, not that she'll need a child to help her remember the man she loved.

"And..." she drew a bracing breath, hoping Gabe would share his confidences if she shared hers "...I was a little angry. Angry at life for being so unfair."

He nodded slowly. "Me, too. I felt all of that, and then some."

"You did? I couldn't tell."

"I did," he assured her. "Just like before."

She finally faced a hard truth. "I was so wrapped up in my own pain that I didn't see yours, did I?"

He sighed. "Neither of us handled our losses well. Let's hope we've learned from our mistakes."

"I also felt something else," she added tentatively. "Disappointment."

"Because you can't get pregnant?"

"No," she said slowly. "I've accepted that. I was disappointed because my husband knew about Theresa's condition and didn't tell me. You don't have to protect me, Gabe. I can handle it."

He met her gaze. "Handle it, how? Like the way you still won't walk past the OB unit after nearly two years?"

Ouch. "Okay, maybe I don't deal with the excitement and joy as well as I should, but it would have been easier for me if I'd been prepared to hear her talk about the baby."

"You're right. I should have mentioned her news."

"You're forgiven," she said lightly. "Frankly, I'm overwhelmed just thinking of what she'll face as she raises this child on her own—dealing with hormones, teenage angst and hi-jinks. It won't be easy."

"She won't be alone," he said. "She'll have plenty of support from her family, Ramon's family, Jack, and all of us who worked with him."

Leah suspected he considered himself a large part of that support, especially when she thought about what he'd done for the single mother-to-be so far. He could say what he wanted, but guilt probably fueled a huge part of his motivation.

"You shouldn't blame yourself, you know."

"I don't. Not about the plane crash, anyway," he corrected. "Who could have known we'd fly into a flock of blasted birds?"

"But you still feel responsible."

He fell silent. "Yes."

At least he'd finally admitted it. "Because you survived and he didn't?"

He fell silent for several long seconds. "He was alive when Jack and I found him, you know. We did everything we could, but he didn't hang on like I begged him to. He just…slipped away."

"I gathered as much from your nightmares, but you're doing a nice thing, Gabe. You established a college fund for his child and paid off his mortgage so his son or daughter would always have a place to live."

"It would have been nicer if I could have saved him."

That, her intuition told her, was really why he was struggling with the tragedy. "You were in the jungle," she reminded him. "Not in a fully equipped emergency department or surgical suite."

"He had so much to live for. Why him? Why Will? Why them and not the rest of us?"

"That's one of the mysteries of life. The thing is, there were three medical professionals at the scene, and one of them was the woman he loved. If he couldn't hang on for her then he physically wasn't able to, and you shouldn't feel as if you failed."

He smiled at her. "For an amateur psychologist, you're a pretty smart gal."

"It's nice of you to notice."

"By the way, we're leaving tomorrow at seven a.m."

She sighed. She'd been hoping he'd had second thoughts about his latest trip. "Then we're still going?"

"Why wouldn't we?"

"Oh, I don't know. I guess because you haven't mentioned a word about it. I thought maybe you'd changed your mind."

"I haven't. Sheldon arranged for the cargo to be loaded today so we'll be ready for takeoff as soon as we arrive at the airport." He studied her a moment. "You really aren't happy about this, are you?"

"No," she said bluntly.

"Why not?"

"One, you seem awfully eager to go. Like you did before."
A cold, foreboding chill ran down her arms. This was the way
the distance between them had first started, and how it had
grown with each subsequent trip. She'd stayed at home with
nothing to occupy herself but her thoughts while he'd jetted
around the world, seemingly without a care.

"Eager isn't the right word. This isn't a holiday."

Her fears churning like Grand Canyon rapids, she began to
pace. "Exactly. You're working and you said you wouldn't."

"Leah—" he began.

She held up her hands to forestall his arguments. "I know.
This is only for three days."

"And it's strictly a mission of mercy," he told her. "Or are
you implying I can't ever respond to a critical need anywhere
ever again?"

"No, but I don't like the way you took away my choice,
Gabe. You reduced this Mexico trip to an obligation, a condition, when it should have been, at the very least, a mutual
decision."

He looked thoughtful, as if he realized his mistake. "Okay,
so I handled that poorly, but I was desperate. I wanted you
with me because I was afraid if I left, even for a few days, I'd
lose my advantage and, ultimately, I'd lose you, too."

"Gabe," she said softly, "we'd already negotiated to spend
the next six weeks together. Did you think so little of me that
I'd renege on our agreement?"

"I couldn't take that chance. Regardless of the way I forced
your cooperation, I really do need you there."

"You need a nurse," she corrected. "Not necessarily
me."

"The nurse I need is you." He leaned forward. "I'm not
looking forward to flying for obvious reasons and I'd travel
another way, if I could. Unfortunately, my other choices aren't
practical or timely. With you beside me, though, I can get on
that plane." He paused. "If I hadn't been coming home—to

you—I doubt if anyone could have forced me to board the last one."

She'd never considered how difficult his return must have been. No doubt every noise had had him thinking the worst. "Oh, Gabe."

"The point is, we have both seen how working with a common purpose builds a team, which is what I want for us. I'm hoping we can accomplish it, but…" He hesitated. "If you truly refuse to join me, I won't stop you."

His offer startled her. "You'd let me stay behind?"

"Yes. According to what I heard this morning, they have a tremendous amount of critically ill children, especially infants. It won't be easy on you."

She didn't know if she should be grateful for his understanding or affronted by the implication that she would be too affected to do her job. More importantly, though, knowing they had so many sick young patients and a shortage of nurses, how could she refuse and still be able to sleep at night? Besides, he had apologized and explained his motivations, misguided though they'd been.

If he'd been so desperate to fix their marriage that he'd resorted to blackmail, then he wasn't simply giving lip service to the idea.

"All right, I'll go." Seeing his suddenly broad smile, she added, "Someone has to make sure you don't overdo it."

"Thanks. You won't regret it."

She already did, not because she didn't want to help those people but because Gabe was obviously expecting more from her than she could give. "I'd better start packing."

He caught up to her before she reached the bottom step. "This could be the thing our relationship needs."

She stared at him with a sad smile. "It might also be the thing that breaks us."

CHAPTER EIGHT

LEAH accompanied Gabe onto the tarmac with mixed emotions. From a medical standpoint she wanted to be a member of his team, but from a personal standpoint she was afraid. He believed working together would foster teamwork and co-operation, and it could. However, it could promote dissension just as easily. This would be a stressful three days for both of them and stress didn't usually bring out the best in people.

Maybe this trip would be a game-changer for their relationship, but if it changed for the worse, it was better they learned it now, rather than later.

However, her thoughts of what might or might not happen faded as soon as she saw how Gabe struggled to climb on board the plane. He drew a deep breath, braced his shoulders and squared his jaw before he finally ducked through the doorway. His hands shook as he buckled his seat belt and on the strength of his reaction she wondered how he'd been able to fly home immediately after his accident.

Helping him cope became her top priority. Throughout the entire flight she held his hand and chatted about everything and anything, asking question after question about Ciuflores. If he noticed she repeated herself, he didn't comment.

Sheldon and Ben, their other team member, obviously anticipated Gabe's reaction, too, because when she was at a loss for words, they took up the slack. The two men kept up a steady stream of chatter through their headsets in a not-so-subtle effort to divert his attention from their position high above ground.

"Try to get some sleep," she advised.

He shot her an are-you-crazy look, but dutifully closed his eyes.

Luckily, the trip went without incident. As soon as the wheels touched down on the level patch of ground that constituted the small airstrip outside Ciuflores, the look of relief sweeping over Gabe's face told how agonizing this trip had been to him. She had to admit to a grudging respect for a man who faced his fears in order to help a friend…

"Thanks for being here," he said simply.

"I'm glad I could help." And she was, she realized. He'd needed her, which thrilled her to the point where she was almost glad she hadn't stayed at home.

Hating the slight tremor in his hands, she kissed his cheek. "Enough lollygagging," she said cheerfully. "It's time to go to work."

As she'd suspected, facing his mission and fulfilling his purpose for being there did wonders for his composure. He squared his shoulders and began issuing orders to Sheldon, Ben and Corey Walsh, their pilot, as he opened the door and exited the plane.

Leah stepped outside the new twin-engined Cessna and was immediately struck by the humidity and the earthy aroma. Flowering trees lined the eastern edge of the clearing, which probably accounted for the floral scent she detected. A hint of something more unpleasant—like the community dump—drifted in from the north, but the thick foliage hid it from view.

A man wearing jeans, a casual shirt and a clerical collar rushed to greet them.

"David!" Gabe exclaimed as he hugged the tall fellow, confirming the priest's identity as Father Odell, Gabe's old classmate who'd established this mission church some seven years earlier. "It's good to see you."

In his late thirties, David had light brown hair and crow's-feet around his eyes, and his skin was tanned from the Mexican sun. He also looked tired but, as Gabe had explained on the plane, David not only ministered to the spiritual needs of the area but also was the director of the only orphanage in the vicinity.

The idea of running across so many parentless children had troubled her, especially as this was the first mention of a local orphans' home, but if Gabe could face his fear of flying, she could deal with the children if it became necessary. She had to because by then she couldn't walk out with the plane at ten thousand feet.

"The feeling is mutual," he answered. "When we heard about your plane crash, I said a lot of masses on your behalf. Then, when you phoned, I could hardly believe our prayers had been answered."

"That makes two of us, David, but with a man of your spiritual pull on my side, how could it have turned out any other way?" he joked.

"All things considered, I didn't expect you to fly here yourself," David chided gently.

"I wouldn't have for anyone except you," Gabe said.

"I'm glad you decided to get back on the horse that threw you, although I wish you'd come under better circumstances."

"Me, too. By the way, this is my wife, Leah."

It was obvious the two were close friends. "Father," she said as she shook his hand. "Gabe has told me so much about you."

"Now, that's a scary thought," the priest teased. "But, please, call me David. What are titles among friends?" He turned back to Gabe. "I assume you brought the supplies Hector requested?"

"And then some," Gabe told him. "If you have a few strong backs, we can start unloading."

David waved forward a group of men standing near the edge of the field. In no time at all the cargo had been moved from the plane to the waiting trucks and they were bouncing their way into town.

Leah clung to Gabe and hoped she'd still have teeth and eardrums when they finally reached their destination.

"Still no shocks on this beast?" Gabe yelled over the noisy muffler.

David grinned. "Why bother with shock absorbers? They'd just wear out. Honestly, though, think of this as nothing more than a free carnival ride."

Because it was futile to talk, the rest of their short trip passed without conversation. Ten minutes later, they reached Ciuflores.

The village's poverty was painfully evident by the dirt-packed streets and ramshackle houses. Grass had long since given up its struggle to survive, although a small patch appeared every now and then. Chickens and dogs roamed freely through the town and goats remained tethered to their owners' yards. What surprised her most was seeing only one person and he had tied a handkerchief over his nose and mouth, bank-robber style.

"Where is everybody?" Gabe asked the same question Leah had on her mind.

"They're staying at home," David explained. "Normally, this is a bustling time of day but with the flu hitting so hard, most aren't venturing out for anything except basic necessities. We're following all precautions but the situation has gotten worse since I called you."

"And your kids?"

Concern spread across David's face. "They fall into three groups. Those who are recovering, those who are currently sick, and those who will probably show symptoms before long. We've also lost four to pneumonia. Because an illness like this spreads through group homes like wildfire, we've sent the sick ones to the hospital to try and contain the illness. Unfortunately, we don't have enough resources to care for everyone, which was why I called you."

He pointed ahead. "This is our clinic, Leah, which we only have because of your husband's generosity."

"And your arm twisting," Gabe added.

David chuckled. "That, too."

The whitewashed building was unassuming and boxlike, in contrast to the graceful Spanish architecture of the neighboring church. Yet even if she hadn't noticed the simple sign in front that read "*Clínica*", it was obvious this was an important building in the community because of the satellite dish perched on the flat roof like an oversize bird.

Inside, four patient wards, which had been designed to hold five patients each, held double that number. Of those, nearly every bed contained a child. One of the rooms was filled with cribs and padded boxes to accommodate the littlest. A few had IV poles standing beside their beds. Some were coughing, some crying, and some were too ill to do either.

In the last room, Dr. Hector Aznar was sitting on a young boy's bed, listening to his lungs. As soon as the nurse beside him murmured in his ear, he looked in their direction and a relieved smile suddenly grew on his face.

"Gabriel, welcome," he said as he approached and shook his hand effusively. "You are a sight to see." He launched into Spanish, which Leah couldn't follow.

Hector seemed to be at least ten years younger than Gabe, but his eyes reflected wisdom and experience that went beyond his years.

As the two men talked, presumably touching on Gabe's accident because Leah understood a few words, she studied her surroundings. One woman in uniform who was obviously a nurse from the way she checked IV bags and listened to lung sounds cared for the twelve toddlers and infants. A few other adults—probably parents—sponged little bodies, held cups and cuddled those who needed cuddling.

"Gabriel says you are a nurse, no?" Hector asked her in his thick accent.

"I am," Leah answered, anticipating his request.

"Good. Any assistance you can give us will be appreciated. Our girls are, shall we say, exhausted."

"I'll do what I can," she said simply. "What strain of influenza are you dealing with?"

He shrugged. "We have not tested anyone, but the ministry of health tells us it is most likely H1N1 Influenza A. Regardless of what name we use, we are fighting an uphill battle. Now that you are here, we can hope to turn the tide, yes?"

"Yes," she said. "Are you the only physician on duty?"

"My partner, Miguel Diego, is here, too, but now that you have arrived, he hopes to travel to the towns we normally visit once a month. Those people are probably in the same dire straits we are but sadly there are more of them than of us."

"Then you have a large caseload," she remarked.

Hector nodded briskly. "Larger than we can adequately care for, but we do our best. Your husband has been what you would call our guardian angel."

Leah stole a glance at her husband. The local physician's praise had brought a tinge of pink to Gabe's face as he grinned sheepishly at her.

Suddenly, all those hours when she'd begrudged his work made her feel extremely small and petty. It was one thing to know her husband's charity made a difference in the lives of so many people and quite another to actually *see* the difference with her own eyes.

Hector spoke rapid-fire Spanish and eventually Gabe nodded before he translated.

"Here's the deal," he began. "Ben, because you're a pediatrician, he would like you to evaluate every child here, starting with the most ill. According to Hector, pneumonia is a real problem so we have to start the IV antibiotics ASAP. The nurses speak English fairly well so you should be okay on your own, but if you run into problems, let me know."

"Okay, but don't wander away too far," Ben said as he shrugged on a gown that Hector provided. "My Spanish is so rusty I could ask for a blood-pressure cuff and get an enema."

Gabe grinned. "Yeah, well, do your best."

As Ben strode off to begin, Leah asked, "Did we bring the IV supplies for—?"

"Pediatric infusion sets are being unpacked as we speak. As soon as we get a handle on the hospitalized, you and I are going on house calls while Hector covers the walk-in cases."

She raised an eyebrow. "Do you really think we're going to accomplish all that today?"

He grinned boyishly, looking far more energized than she'd expected, considering his emotionally and physically stressful journey. She was feeling overwhelmed and she'd slept on the plane for a few hours, whereas Gabe had hardly closed his eyes. "Welcome to my world."

After one of the nurses shyly identified herself as Elena, she steered Leah to her first patient—a three-year-old girl who cried fitfully but sucked greedily on the bottle Elena handed her.

"It is electrolyte drink. She is not as sick as others but now you are here, she will have IV, too. If you would sponge her down, please?"

Leah saw how the little girl lacked the strength to hold her own bottle. Immediately, she sat in the nearby chair, cradled the child in her arms and held the bottle. As the child relaxed against her, she brushed away the sweat-dampened dark curls from her forehead.

"Where are her parents?" she asked Elena, who was wringing out a wet rag in a nearby basin of iced water.

"At home with their other children," she answered, handing the cloth to Leah. "They are sick, too, but not as sick as Sofita." She stared down at Leah and smiled. "She rests. Good. When bottle *está vacío*, go to next."

At the rate Sofita was guzzling the fluid, it wouldn't take long for her to finish. In the meantime, Leah propped the drink against her chest and held it in place with the same arm she'd crooked around the child's head. With her right hand, she ran the cool cloth over her face and arms.

The small sigh of obvious pleasure and the twitch of a smile were all the thanks Leah needed.

A short time later, she gently laid the toddler in her crib. After washing her hands, she moved to the next patient, as Elena had instructed. The Spanish nurse had placed IV sets in or near every bed, and with her help they began inserting the lines into tiny veins. Most of the children were too ill to give more than a token protest, which threatened Leah's composure more than once. As soon as they had the fluids and antibiotics running, she gave each one a bottle, a cuddle and a cooling sponge bath.

Time didn't matter. Caring for these kids did.

Finally, she reached a five-year-old boy who was so severely dehydrated she couldn't raise a vein. When he hardly flinched at her failed attempts, she knew she was in trouble.

"How's it going?" Gabe asked. His timing couldn't have been more perfect.

"Thank goodness you're here," she said, frustrated. "He's so dehydrated I can't start his IV. I've tried twice and I can't poke him again. I was hoping you'd try."

"Okay." Gabe took her place on the bed and began his search for a suitable site. When he'd succeeded and the IV fluid dripped at a steady pace, Leah wanted to cheer.

"Are you ready for a break?" he asked.

She stared at him, horrified by his suggestion. "I'm not finished. I still have IVs to start and—"

"This is the last one," he told her gently. "See?"

She finally glanced around the room and, sure enough, an IV bag hung near every bed.

"But I haven't cuddled this one yet," she said. "Or bathed him, or—"

"I will do that, Señora Montgomery," Elena came up to say. "We have done well. Go with your husband."

"But you've worked longer than I have."

"Go." Elena tugged her away from the bed. "I will sit as I watch Felipe."

"Come on, Leah," Gabe coaxed. "You won't be much of use if you wear yourself out on the first day."

Reluctantly, she followed him. "Where are we going?"

"To eat," he said, leading her past the patient areas to an average-sized room that served as Hector's office and staff lounge. There, two covered plates of food were waiting, along with a pot of rich black coffee.

"Hmm," Gabe said, sniffing the air and whipping the napkins off the plates. "This smells like Carlotta's cooking. She makes the best tamales, beans and rice." His hand froze and a thoughtful expression crossed his face.

"Carlotta? Is this the woman you suspect has pancreatic cancer? The one who cares for her three grandchildren?"

"Yes."

"If she's in the kitchen, maybe she isn't as ill as you thought."

"Maybe. When I have a minute, I'll find out."

At first, Leah thought she was too keyed up to eat, but the delightful aroma convinced her otherwise. She tasted the beans while Gabe poured two mugs of coffee.

"Has everyone else eaten?" she asked as he rejoined her at the table for four.

"I assume so. We took the last two places."

"Is it always like this when you visit a place?" she asked.

"The experience is never quite the same," he said. "We've conducted clinics before and treated a lot more people, but never this many seriously ill cases at once."

"I almost feel as if I'm in the middle of a disaster drill, except this isn't a practice. These children are really sick. I haven't stopped until now and I haven't stepped out of the one ward."

"What's sad is how the patients in the other three are just as ill, if not more so."

"You realize that three days isn't nearly enough time to make a dent in treating these people?"

"Believe me, no one is more aware of that than I. What's more disconcerting is when you realize Ciuflores isn't the only village experiencing this scenario. What we're seeing is taking place across the country. A lot of those communities aren't as lucky as this one."

The picture he'd painted wasn't pretty.

"Because they don't have a Father David who has a personal connection to the CEO of a charitable organization?" she asked.

His mouth curved into a gentle smile. "Exactly."

Gabe polished off the food on his plate then leaned back. "Are you hinting you'd like to stay longer?"

Was she? "I'm only making an observation," she said. "But isn't it difficult to leave when you know your work isn't finished?"

"Definitely," he agreed, "but staying until the crisis ends isn't feasible. Hector and his staff know that, and they're grateful for every bit of help we provide because it's more than they had before. When you stop to think about it, Ben and I have literally doubled the number of medical professionals in a sixty-mile radius, so we can treat twice as many patients. We may be a mere stitch in a wound that needs ten, but sometimes one, if properly placed, is better than nothing."

He stared at her now empty plate. "Are you ready to tackle our next assignment, Nurse Montgomery?"

She was starting to get her second wind. "Sure."

"Good, because, house calls, here we come."

Armed with David and his knowledge of his parishioners, Gabe began his round of house calls. He found everything from a household with only one or two sick individuals to homes where the entire family was symptomatic. Fortunately, none required hospitalization, which was good because he didn't know where Hector and his staff would squeeze in another patient.

Leah, however, was a star in his eyes. She performed basic

nursing care from taking temperatures to giving sponge baths. She taught children and parents to sneeze into the crooks of their arms and, with David's helpful translation skills, encouraged them to wash their hands with soap and water for the same length of time it took to sing the happy birthday song.

As soon as it was too dark to see more than a few feet in front of them, Leah was lagging behind and even David appeared a little frayed around the edges. Gabe wasn't functioning on much more than adrenalin, either.

"We're calling it a night," he told his crew as they returned to David's truck.

"We can see a few more people," Leah protested.

"We could," he agreed, "but we won't. We're all exhausted and tomorrow is another day."

Leah dutifully climbed into the cab of the truck, allowing the two men relative privacy.

"Your wife doesn't know when to quit, does she?" David asked.

"Afraid not."

"Have you told her where you two are bunking down?"

Gabe should have, but the opportunity hadn't presented itself until now. "Not yet. I'm hoping she'll be too tired to care."

"Good luck with that. If we weren't having an epidemic, I could make other arrangements, but—"

"We'll be fine at the orphanage," Gabe said firmly, hoping he was right. "Leah will understand our choices are limited. Did you find places for Sheldon, Ben and Corey, our pilot?"

"They're bunking together down the hall. I'm sorry I only had two rooms to spare, one for you and your wife and one for the others."

"We won't spend that much time in them anyway," Gabe answered practically.

"True. By the way, in the morning, before you're torn in a hundred different directions, save a few minutes for me, okay?"

"A problem?"

David sighed. "Yes and no. It's too late to go into detail."

"I'll find you first thing," Gabe promised.

As it happened, Leah was too exhausted to notice her surroundings, or, if she did, the fact simply didn't register. Gabe gratefully ushered her into the room they'd been given, although he knew his moment of reckoning would come in the morning.

As soon as she saw the bed, she sighed gratefully and began stripping off her clothes. By the time Gabe had opened his duffle bag, Leah was curled beneath the covers.

"Sweet dreams," he said softly, but she was already fast asleep.

He undressed down to boxers and a T-shirt and slipped under the sheet beside her. Immediately, she snuggled against him and he tucked her under his arm, pleased she'd turned to him without being aware of it. Which only proved that subconsciously she knew she belonged at his side.

Holding her against him, Gabe reflected on their day. She'd been such a godsend. Not only had she kept him sane on their long flight, she'd been a great partner when they'd finally started to work. She'd anticipated his requests, offered suggestions, and both her smile and calm manner had soothed the most anxious parents and fretful kids. He'd accomplished a lot today and he owed it all to her.

As he began drifting off, he realized her presence had given him another benefit. Normally, on trips such as these, he had a hard time going to sleep. Between pushing himself to the point where he was simply too tired to doze off and thinking of everything he had to accomplish the next day, he had trouble shutting off his brain so his body could follow suit.

Now, though, having her in his arms, listening to her gentle breathing and feeling her steady heartbeat brought him peace.

Tomorrow would start early and end late, but one good thing had happened already as a result of their trip.

After so many months apart, Leah was finally sharing his bed.

CHAPTER NINE

A THUMP and a giggle teased Leah as she dreamed of a summertime picnic with three children. Another giggle, a loud whisper, a foot digging into her side and a happy-sounding "Shhh" jarred the pleasant scene in her head, and she slowly opened her eyes. The two little girls straddling Gabe's chest in their nightgowns startled her completely awake.

"What in the world—?"

"She is awake?" the oldest asked, and immediately a boy, who looked to be about four years old and was wearing cowboy-print pajamas, climbed aboard, too.

The youngsters all chattered a mile a minute at Gabe, who simply laughed and answered in Spanish. Although she couldn't follow the conversation, she recognized a few words—*desayuno*, breakfast, and *señora*, lady.

"Gabe?" she asked as the smallest girl suddenly leaned over Leah and smiled at her around the thumb in her mouth. "What's going on?"

"This is Anna, Rosa and José. They are Carlotta's grandchildren," he explained as he sat up, holding on to Rosa so she didn't tumble off the mattress. "Anna is the oldest. She's five. Rosa is almost two and José is four."

"Carlotta the cook?"

"Yeah. They all live here with the rest of the kids."

"The *rest* of the kids?" she echoed. "Where *are* we?"

"David gave us a room in the staff quarters at the orphanage."

"We're staying in the *orphanage*?" she asked, horrified.

"I know what you're thinking, but this is where we usually bunk down. Besides, David couldn't ask a family who's sick to take us in."

She exhaled, knowing she couldn't refute his logic. She could do this. She *would*.

"Fine, but do we have to stay in the same room?"

"David only had two available. We have one and the rest of our group is sharing the other."

"I don't suppose we can ask for another bed or a cot?"

"All extra beds and cots are being used by patients. Unless you'd like to kick one of them off their mattress so you can have one to yourself?"

She cast him a disgusted look. "Of course not," she grumbled. "Maybe one of us should sleep on the floor."

"Feel free," he said. "I'm the one with the sore ribs, remember? Besides, nothing will happen in here that you don't want to happen."

His comment wasn't completely consoling. Given the opportunity—and her own weakness where he was concerned—they'd do far more than sleep. The good news was that they'd probably both be too exhausted when they finally fell into bed to have the energy to make love.

Just then the children bounced on Gabe again as each one chattered louder than the other in an obvious attempt to get his attention.

So much for his sore ribs, she thought uncharitably, eying the youngsters. Yet their excitement was contagious. After seeing the seriously ill children yesterday, it was refreshing to see such happy, healthy ones.

"I'm sorry about the early wake-up call." He tugged on the oldest girl's pigtail. "The kids aren't supposed to barge in, but they'd heard I'd arrived and, well…" he shrugged helplessly "…they couldn't wait to see us."

He tickled José and the dark-haired imp laughed with delight.

"You have an exuberant fan club," she remarked.

Gabe's grin made him look like the man in their wedding photos. The shadow she'd seen in his eyes yesterday had lifted and joy shone in its place as he tugged on José's hair. "I'm a novelty," he said.

Leah watched as Anna leaned over and planted a sloppy kiss on Gabe's cheek. "For being a novelty, they're very comfortable around you." In fact, she thought they were more than comfortable—they all looked at Gabe as if he was their personal fairy godfather.

"They remember me from my previous trips and haven't forgotten that I usually bring candy."

Rosa's eyes sparkled with interest. *"¿Tienes chocolate?"*

"Later," Gabe promised, as he threw back the sheet and swung his feet onto the floor. "After breakfast."

Immediately the children screeched with delight. His next words sent the children scampering off the bed with several more enthusiastic bounces before they disappeared through the open door.

"What did you tell them?" she asked.

"Candy is for children who eat their oatmeal first. I also reminded them that Father David won't be happy if their grandmother reported them missing."

"Well, I guess this means we should get up and start the day, though I still feel like I need another few hours in bed!"

"Did you sleep well?"

"I must have. I don't remember a thing after I stumbled in here last night."

"I'm not surprised. You worked hard yesterday. Unfortunately, today won't be easier."

"I didn't expect a vacation when I left home," she told him. "So don't apologize."

"Okay." He rose and stretched. "Come on, lazybones. Breakfast and our adoring public are waiting."

The morning meal was a noisy affair. The trestle tables were full of youngsters of varying ages, all waiting for their food. Yet when David rose to say the blessing, the littlest to the oldest became so quiet Leah could have heard a mouse scamper across the floor.

While Sheldon and Gabe discussed their plans for the day—Ben apparently had spent the night at the clinic to monitor several patients who'd needed ventilator support—Leah sensed she was being watched. At first, she disregarded her suspicion because so many of the children kept glancing in their direction, but the feeling persisted. When she saw the trio of children who'd provided their early-morning wake-up call, she knew she hadn't been imagining things.

Rosa was studying her with a thoughtful expression and José watched Gabe with adoration. Anna's gaze drifted from Gabe to her, then back to Gabe again, and it held such longing that it nearly undid her.

There was no doubt about it. For whatever reason, these children loved Gabe. And seeing the sparkle in their eyes when they captured his attention made her realize how she, too, had once looked at him through those same eyes of love.

Curious about the children's story, she waited to ask until the meal was over and Gabe had left the table to deliver the promised treat. While he was swarmed over by the youngsters, she pressed David for answers.

"Their grandmother has been our cook ever since her husband died several years ago," David began. "After her son and daughter-in-law were killed when his fishing boat capsized about a year ago, the children came to live with Carlotta. She needed to keep her job to support herself, so we worked out an arrangement where she continued to cook at a slightly reduced salary in exchange for day care and a place for the three of them to live."

He sighed. "The really unfortunate thing is that Carlotta has recently been diagnosed with pancreatic cancer."

"Gabe suspected as much but I didn't realize her diagnosis was official."

"Unfortunately—her condition being what it is—we don't know how much longer she'll be with us."

Leah's heart went out to the three children. To lose their parents and, soon, their grandmother… Life would be tough for them. "I'm so sorry to hear that. Do they have any other family?"

"Carlotta has another son. The children's uncle. We're trying to locate him, but no one seems to know where he is, what he's doing, or if he's even alive. I've been told he was quite a hellion in his younger days and went to Mexico City, where he fell in with the wrong crowd. Carlotta hasn't heard from him in years."

"What happens to them, then, after…?"

"If we can't find their next of kin, they'll stay here. If we do find their uncle, the children will go with him, unless he doesn't want them." He sighed. "The odds aren't in favor of him accepting the responsibility, but it's hard to say what might happen."

Leah glanced at the children interspersed around the room. "I presume all the children have a similarly sad story."

He shrugged. "More or less. Some are orphans, others have parents who simply can't provide for them."

"They're all from Ciuflores?"

"No. We're the only orphanage in the area, so kids come here from miles around. If I had the space, we could easily double our number. Life in this part of the country is difficult and the children often pay the price."

"I see." She paused, watching the three as they clung to Gabe, but it was more for his attention than the candy he provided. "Those three seem to love Gabe," she remarked.

"They all do," David said simply, "although I have to admit he has a special rapport with these kids in particular. Their faces always light up when I mention his name. I'm not sure why because he doesn't single them out but I suppose it's the same for them as it is with us. There are some people we feel more comfortable with than others.

"The thing is, he's good with children, in general," David continued. "A modern-day Pied Piper. He definitely has a gift."

"He does," she agreed, trying to ignore the sudden ache his words caused in her chest. If not for her, Gabe would have a houseful of his own children.

A sudden scuffle at the opposite end of the dining room drew the priest's attention. Either he had eyes at the back of his head or being the director of an orphanage of fifty had given him a sixth sense for trouble. "Sorry for deserting you," David apologized, "but I have to play referee."

David hurried toward the two teenagers, who were shoving each other and occasionally throwing punches. Rather than observe the drama unfolding at that end of the room, she watched Gabe as he dug in his pockets and passed pieces of wrapped hard candy to the children who swarmed him.

He looked so happy as he laughed, joked and hefted the littlest ones into the air.

She thought of the instances when they'd visited friends with children or her own family gatherings with her sister's kids. Their children had always climbed over Gabe on their arrival and she'd attributed their attraction to his freely lavished and complete attention.

His affinity for little people didn't stop there, either. Sick children responded to his smile and quiet confidence in a way that many adults did not. She'd seen that scenario more often than not in the hospital. More recently, she'd seen it during yesterday's house calls.

David's description of Pied Piper seemed apt.

Her insecurities suddenly flooded over her. It was far too easy to wonder if Gabe regretted marrying her or if he wished he'd cooperated when she'd offered a divorce. A legal piece of paper would have given him the freedom to find someone who could fill the need for a child in his life.

Although she rapidly dismissed those ideas as foolishness because he'd said he would love her regardless, one hard truth stared at her.

She was the one holding up the adoption process. *She* was the roadblock to their dreams of a family. Gabe had given control over those dreams to her, and *she* now carried the deciding vote.

Don't let fear influence your choice.

Deep in her thoughts, she didn't notice Rosa had toddled over to her until she felt a small hand on her knee.

Leah stiffened, an instinctive reaction born from her reluctance to let herself grow too close to a child…*any* child…but the trust shining in those dark brown eyes and the featherlight touch that was both comforting and tentative made her smile come easily.

"Shouldn't you be with your grandmother?" Leah asked. Then, because the little girl didn't seem to understand, she fished for the right phrases in her limited vocabulary. *"¿Dónde está tu abuelita?"* Where is your grandmother? *"Debes estar con ella."* You should be with her.

Rosa simply popped a thumb into her mouth and grinned.

Unable to stop herself, Leah stroked the tousled jet-black curls. "Don't you want to play with your friends?"

Rosa didn't answer. Instead, she simply waited, as if she had faith in Leah's ability to eventually figure out what she wanted.

Oh, please, let something else grab her attention, Leah thought. It was one thing to share her love with nieces and nephews and quite another to give it to a child she'd never see again. And yet she couldn't send Rosa away, not when she was waiting so patiently for acknowledgment. This toddler had already known more rejection than any child at her age should. She wouldn't add to it.

"Do you want me to hold you?" Leah asked. She searched her limited vocabulary for the proper phrase and came up missing. She simply patted her lap and held out her hands.

As if Rosa had been waiting for the invitation, she immediately popped her thumb out of her mouth, climbed up and made herself comfortable.

With an awkwardness that came more out of emotional

uncertainty rather than a lack of the mechanics involved, Leah shifted positions to tuck Rosa under her arm.

With her thumb back in her mouth, Rosa melted against her, as if there wasn't another place she'd rather be.

Certain one of the staff would soon retrieve the toddler, Leah allowed herself to enjoy the weight of the little body in her lap and the special scent so common to babies. Slowly, tentatively, she began to rub her shoulder.

"I wonder what you're thinking," Leah said, aware that even if Rosa understood her, she couldn't answer. "You are definitely a snuggler, aren't you?"

Rosa smiled around her thumb as if she understood or was simply happy to have Leah all to herself.

"I'll bet you've wrapped Father David and everyone else around your little finger," she murmured.

It wouldn't have been difficult to do, she decided. She'd been holding the tyke for less than five minutes and already felt the gossamer ties ensnaring her.

Somewhat amazed by Rosa's decision to seek her out, Leah simply continued to hold her and savor the moments when suddenly Anna and José appeared beside her. He held out a small battered toy truck while Anna showed off her own precious possession, a doll that showed it had obviously been well loved by the threadbare dress, broken nose and missing index finger. Immediately, Rosa squirmed off Leah's lap and disappeared as fast as her short legs would take her.

Wondering what had sent Rosa away, Leah admired the other children's toys. "Does your truck make a noise?" she asked José, then made a few questioning engine sounds. The boy beamed and he knelt down to run the truck beside her feet to demonstrate.

While he was occupied, Leah touched the doll's face. "Does your doll have a name?" she asked. *"¿Nombre?"*

Anna's smile stretched from ear to ear. "Sarita," she answered, before launching into a conversation that Leah couldn't begin to follow. It obviously revolved around Sarita because Anna stroked what was left of her doll's pigtails.

Suddenly, a new lovey was thrust into her lap—a light brown teddy bear with matted fur, a frayed red neck ribbon and one eye. Apparently Rosa wasn't to be outdone because she waited for Leah to acknowledge her toy, too.

Conflicting emotions filled Leah's chest—pain that these children were so happy with so little, and awe that they wanted to share what obviously meant so much to them. Plus, they wanted to share it with *her*.

For an instant she couldn't breathe and her vision blurred. She was desperate to escape and began frantically looking around the dining hall for Gabe to rescue her, but Anna spoke and Leah knew she couldn't obey her instinct to run away. Leaving the three so abruptly would be a rejection they couldn't understand and didn't deserve.

So she forced herself to breathe slowly and deeply until the overwhelming feeling passed, leaving bittersweet longing in its wake.

If not for David's intervention, Gabe would never have been able to untangle himself from the children clamoring for his attention. Fortunately, after David had dealt with the two boys who'd clearly experienced a difference of opinion, he clapped his hands and ordered the children to their daily chores. Less than thirty seconds later, the noise level had dropped considerably and he saw Carlotta slowly approach, leaning heavily on the girl beside her.

"Shouldn't you be in bed?" He fussed over the woman, who didn't appear anything like she had when he'd last seen her. She'd lost weight and her skin color reflected the toll her cancer was taking on her. Perhaps if he'd been able to convince her to go to a major facility for tests when he'd first examined her, they might have been able to halt the disease and give her a bit more time, but now it was too late. According to David, Taylor had talked Hector through a biopsy procedure and a preliminary result had confirmed the aggressive nature of her disease. While surgery and subsequent chemotherapy were options, those treatments would only prolong the inevitable.

"I will go there soon enough," Carlotta told him with a smile as she accepted the chair he'd pulled out for her then tiredly waved away her helper. "I must do what I can now. Your breakfast was good?"

According to David, Carlotta had been teaching two girls to take her place in the kitchen. From the food Gabe had eaten so far, Carlotta's replacements were learning their lessons well.

"It was delicious, as was yesterday's meal," he answered.

"Good. I want to see my grandchildren. They seem happy, yes?"

Gabe turned to find his wife and saw her surrounded by the three familiar faces. For a moment he waited and watched the childless woman with three motherless children...and wished.

"Your wife has a mother's touch."

"She does."

"Yet, the padre says you do not have children."

He ignored the familiar twinge of disappointment. "We had a little boy, but he was too small when he was born. Then we tried to adopt, but things didn't work out. So, no, we don't have children of our own."

"I see. That explains why your wife isn't, what is the word, *comfortable* with my babies? She has too much pain inside."

"Probably."

"And yet she has a good heart."

"She does." Gabe watched as Leah planted a kiss against José's temple. As he squirmed, she laughed as if she found his reaction humorous.

"You carry your own sorrow, do you not, Dr. Gabriel?"

He hesitated. "A part of me always will," he said simply. Then, because he wasn't comfortable under the older woman's scrutiny, he motioned toward the scene before them. "Your grandchildren are great kids."

"Even when they wake you early?"

He chuckled. "You knew they'd paid us a visit?"

"Grandmothers have eyes everywhere."

"With those three, you need them," he said.

"Oh, yes." Her gaze drifted in Leah's direction and she smiled at José's demonstration of his truck. "He is my busy one," she said. "Always moving, even in his sleep. Anna is my noisy one because she talks, talks, talks. And Rosa…" Her face was a mixture of love and sorrow as Rosa rested in Leah's lap. "Rosa is my cuddly one. It is good they are familiar with everyone here."

"No one will ever take your place," he said kindly, "regardless of who cares for them."

"Thank you for that, Dr. Gabriel," she whispered. "You, too, have a good heart. Perhaps Father David will find someone like you and your wife to take my place."

Gabe froze. Was Carlotta hinting that she wanted Gabe to adopt her grandchildren? If so, would Leah be open to the idea, especially after she'd adamantly refused to adopt? As he glanced at the children, he admitted that in spite of telling Leah he'd abide by her decision he'd love nothing more than to take these children into their home. He truly wanted to make it happen—to barge in, full steam ahead, just as she'd accused him of doing—but he couldn't. He'd told her the choice was hers, and he'd stick by that, even if it killed him.

"Do not fret," Carlotta told him. "What will be, will be." She struggled to her feet. "Come. Those three will play all day with your wife if we let them. Shall we rescue her?"

CHAPTER TEN

LEAH knew they were pushing hard to see as many patients as possible because they were scheduled to fly home in the morning. She hated leaving when the residents of this community obviously needed her help and she consoled herself with the reminder that the assistance she'd provided had eased the regular staff's burden to a small degree.

She also had to admit that the Salazar children had captured her heart, and in such a short time, too. How could they not, especially when Rosa smiled hugely whenever she saw her, then toddled over and wanted to be held?

These aren't your children, Leah told herself as she played with Anna and José. *You're just—what did Gabe call it? A novelty. Yes. That's it.*

In one small corner of her mind she was glad they were leaving so soon. She didn't want them to become so entrenched in her affections that her departure would be traumatic. They'd have enough to deal with when their grandmother died because they were old enough to remember her—at least for a while—but too young to understand why the one constant in their lives had disappeared forever.

During her odd moments she wished she could take all three home with her, but it was impossible. Their uncle would assume responsibility, which was as it should be.

By mid-afternoon, she had lost track of the number of homes they had visited. Most had at least one parent healthy enough to care for the sick members of their household, but the very last family they visited—the Ortiz family—was in dire straits. Every member was ill and the mother, pregnant with her third child, had an advanced case of pneumonia. The father had left several weeks earlier to find work and no one knew when he would return.

Leah, David and Gabe stood off in one corner to discuss their options.

"We can't leave her here," Leah warned. "She has diminished lung capacity with the baby pressing on her diaphragm. She needs to be in the hospital with round-the-clock nursing care, not to mention ventilator support."

"The hospital is full," Gabe pointed out.

"But if she stays at home…" Leah left her sentence unsaid. The outcome, in her opinion, was obvious.

"I know," Gabe said tiredly. "She won't make it for sure."

"Then David will increase his occupancy by two, at least in the short term."

"He still might," he warned. "Being in the hospital doesn't mean we'll provide a magical cure."

She knew as well as anyone how hard this strain of influenza was on pregnant women. "Yes, but there she has a fighting chance. Left at home, she has none."

Her argument had its desired influence because Gabe turned to David. "What will we do with the children if we can find a bed for her? Can you find someone to stay with them?"

"Ordinarily, I'd say yes, but I'm running out of healthy adults," David said ruefully. "The best I can do is bring them to the orphanage."

"But won't we expose the others?" Leah asked, hating the thought of Rosa and the other children contracting the same disease.

"We'll quarantine them," Gabe said.

"But David doesn't have enough staff to separate these two from the rest," she protested.

He raised an eyebrow. "What do you want me to do,

Leah? The hospital doesn't have room—we're going to have to squeeze her in as it is—and we can't leave them here to fend for themselves."

"We have no choice," David added. "We'll do the best we can and pray it will be enough."

She exhaled, hating their lack of options. "You're right. Just be sure your staff understands how easily the flu can spread through the orphanage if they aren't careful."

"I'm counting on you to remind them," he said.

"Then it's settled," Gabe said. "We'll move her to the hospital and the children to the orphanage."

As they turned to leave, Leah held Gabe back while David went on ahead to make arrangements. "How are you doing?"

"Fine."

"You look tired."

His smile was lopsided. "Aw, honey, I'm way past tired, but thanks for asking."

"Maybe you should take a break."

"I can't. Not now. Not with Mrs. Ortiz in her condition." He rubbed his face.

"You're worried about her," she guessed.

"I'm worried about a lot of things," he admitted. "Can we help her pull through with limited resources? Can we give her the attention she needs when so many others need it, too? Frankly, how Hector and Miguel bear up under this on a daily basis boggles my mind."

"Maybe the epidemic will play itself out soon."

"We can always hope." He dropped a quick kiss on her mouth then straightened as he gave her a rueful smile. "Gotta run."

A short time later, Leah found herself not only selecting a room for the two far away from the others but also instructing all the adults and older children on proper hygiene. Through it all, Carlotta's grandchildren became her shadows, although she refused to allow them in the same room as the sick children. A few times she was certain she'd caught a glimpse of

Carlotta out of the corner of her eye, but when she looked, the woman was gone.

Leah felt guilty for enjoying Rosa and Anna's attention, especially when she knew their time with their grandmother was so short, but having three energetic children in the older woman's sickroom wouldn't be a pleasant experience for any of them. She was doing the woman a favor by looking after the three, she told herself. After tomorrow, someone else would take over, anyway. Until then she planned to store up memories of toothy smiles, sloppy kisses and gentle hugs.

Dinner was a semi-relaxed affair, eaten in the dining hall long after the children had finished and were playing outside. David had disappeared into his office and Sheldon and Ben were back at the clinic, leaving Gabe and Leah to enjoy another meal of tamales and beans.

"I can't believe we're going home tomorrow," she remarked.

"Time flies when you're having fun."

She reached across the table to cover his hand. "I wouldn't call this fun. I'd describe the trip as enlightening, challenging and overwhelming."

"But you're glad you came."

She nodded slowly. "I am."

"We make a pretty good team, don't we?"

"Is this where you say, 'I told you so'?" she asked lightly, aware that so far this trip seemed to be fulfilling Gabe's expectations. Working together had opened her eyes to many things, but most of all she'd finally been able to see Gabe's character without the vision being distorted by her own pain and resentment. In fact, she was seeing the man she'd fallen in love with and knew it wouldn't take much to push her over the edge.

"I hear the garden has a beautiful moonlit path," he said offhandedly. "Want to check it out with me tonight?"

"A moonlight stroll sounds perfect. Do you think we can disappear for a while, though?"

"I don't see why not. Everything seems to be under control."

Sheldon took that moment to approach and lean over the table. His face was solemn, his tone grave as he spoke. "You spoke too soon, boss. We have a problem."

Gabe's shoulders slumped slightly. From Leah's own experience with Gabe's second-in-command, Sheldon tended toward understatement rather than exaggeration. If he said there was a problem then the problem was usually major, not minor.

"Somehow, I'm not surprised," Gabe said wryly. "What's up?"

"Ben wants you in the hospital ASAP."

Gabe frowned. "We were just there. Did he say why?"

"Not really. Something about Hector."

Leah exchanged a glance with Gabe. "What could be wrong with him?"

Gabe rose. "Let's find out."

They found the clinic's physician lying on the small cot in his office. Ben was sitting beside him as he listened to Hector's ragged breathing while Elena sponged off his face in an obvious attempt to bring down his fever.

"What happened?" Gabe asked in a low voice.

Ben slung his stethoscope around his neck and motioned them into the hallway. "Influenza."

Gabe's heart sank. "Damn," he muttered, running his hands through his hair. "We don't need this on top of everything else."

"My sentiments exactly," Ben agreed. "I noticed he wasn't feeling well this morning, but he shrugged it off as exhaustion from too-long days and too-short nights. Then, about thirty minutes ago, he could hardly stay on his feet and wasn't making any sense when he talked. I thought maybe it was the language barrier, so I found Elena to talk to him. She was as clueless as I was."

Elena nodded, her dark eyes large with worry. "*Sí.* He was

out of his head, talking crazy talk." She made circular motions near her ear.

"Elena and I convinced him to go to bed, which didn't take too much effort, I might add. Then I sent Sheldon to find you." He hesitated. "We're going to need a Plan B."

Gabe pinched the bridge of his nose, already anticipating the repercussions Hector's illness would have. From the looks on everyone's faces, they were realizing them, too.

He turned to Elena. "Do you know when Dr. Diego will return? Is there any way we can reach him before then?"

"He will be back in a week, maybe more, maybe less." She shrugged helplessly. "I can send someone to find him, but he does not always follow the same path. Sometimes he goes here first. Sometimes there first. Is no way to tell."

"What about a cell phone?"

She shook her head. "It does not work where he is going."

Damn! Gabe felt everyone's gaze as they waited for his answer. He only wished he had one to give.

"Here are our options," he said. "We leave as scheduled—"

Leah gasped. "But we can't desert these people now, when they don't have a doctor and they're in the middle of a medical crisis. Even if the patients were all doing well, the nurses can't handle Mrs. Ortiz—the pregnant woman we brought in earlier."

"Or…" he cast a meaningful glance at her for interrupting "…we stay until Miguel returns, which could be a week or more. And that will affect our other commitments." He turned to Sheldon. "The clinic in Tennessee comes to mind."

"Don't forget the trip to Alaska," Sheldon reminded him.

Sensing Leah was about to explode with frustration, he glanced at Ben. "Your anniversary is a few days away, if I remember correctly."

Ben cleared his throat and looked apologetic. "Yeah. My wife planned a big party. It's our tenth, and I promised I'd be there," he said to Leah as she was the only one who hadn't heard.

Gabe glanced at Sheldon. "How are the supplies holding out?"

"We've used about two-thirds of what we brought," Sheldon admitted. "Under normal conditions for a community this size, what's left should last a while. But…" he shrugged "…these aren't normal conditions. Everything depends on how near we are to the end of this outbreak."

"What's your opinion, Ben?" Gabe asked. "Are we on the downhill slope?"

"You've seen as many if not more patients than I have," the other physician replied. "If I had to guess, from the number and severity of the cases who've landed in the clinic, I'd say we're still in the thick of things."

Gabe agreed, although he'd hoped Ben might have drawn a different conclusion. "Then we have a third option."

"Which is?" Leah asked.

"I'll stay behind while the rest of you head back as originally planned. Sheldon, you handle the business end of sending down another shipment. Corey can help."

Sheldon nodded. "I'll get back as soon as I can." He grinned. "If not before."

"I'm staying, too," Leah declared, her chin rising defiantly. "I may not be a physician, but I can help."

She'd be a welcome addition, but he wasn't worried about her ability to hold their pace. He had three objections to her remaining behind, and they were all under the age of six. "Yes, but—"

"If you're not going home, neither am I."

Knowing she wouldn't appreciate an argument in front of everyone, he simply shot her his best we'll-talk-about-it-later look. To her credit, she didn't say a word, but her eyes promised a heated discussion.

He turned to his team. "Then it's settled. You two will fly back in the morning. Sheldon, you'll return as soon as you can arrange for another supply shipment."

"Piece of cake," Sheldon boasted.

"In that case," Ben said, "I'll take tonight's shift. This may be the only night you'll get any sleep."

It probably would be. After Ben climbed aboard their plane, Gabe would be on duty twenty-four seven.

"Okay, but call if you get more than you can handle."

Throughout the rest of their conversation, Leah didn't say a word, which didn't bode well. Still, Gabe hoped their moonlight walk through the garden would help as it could easily be the only private time he'd enjoy with her until they flew back to the U.S.

As soon as he'd finished hammering out last-minute details with Sheldon, he grabbed Leah's arm and led her out of the clinic. Darkness had fallen and the usual nighttime noises surrounded them as he walked beside her to the orphanage.

She held herself stiffly under the guiding hand he'd placed at the small of her back.

"Nice evening, isn't it?" he asked, making conversation to soften her irritation.

"Hmm."

He glanced at the building looming ahead, noticing the bank of windows in the orphanage's dormitory wing was dark. "Looks like the kids are all in bed."

"I'd say so."

She'd said a complete sentence; he was making progress.

"The garden's around the back," he said. "Watch your step. The ground is uneven." He took her hand before he led her down a small footpath and held back shrubs and branches for her to pass by unscathed. Finally, they arrived in a clearing that boasted a stone bench and a multitude of flowers. The colors were muted in the moonlight, but the white blooms seemed to glow as if nature had saved their beauty for midnight lovers. Their fragrance filled the air with a heady, sensual perfume.

"Oh, Gabe," she breathed as she turned a complete circle. "This is beautiful."

Relieved at how their surroundings had broken through

her reserve, Gabe smiled. "Not as beautiful as the woman standing here."

She met his gaze. "Do you really think so?"

"I know so." He traced a line from her temple down to her jaw.

"Then why...?" She bit her lip in indecision. "Why don't you want me to stay here with you?"

The hurt in her voice was as painful to hear as it obviously was for her to say. "I want you to stay," he confessed, "because I like having you here. It simply isn't in your best interests."

"Don't yo-yo on me, Gabe," she warned. "Why isn't it in my best interests? After all the fuss you made to get me here, now you insist I go? And without you?" She shook her head. "I don't understand."

"You're growing too attached to Carlotta's grandchildren and you've only been around them for a couple of days. How hard will it be on you to leave after another week?"

"Yes, I'm fond of them. They're sweet kids." She spoke as if she weighed each word beforehand. "You're trying to protect me again but it isn't necessary. When we finally go home, I'll handle it."

"Are you sure?" Perhaps it was his job to be supportive instead of doubtful, but he wanted Leah to know exactly what she would face. "Leaving these kids won't be like leaving your nieces and nephews. Chances are you'll never see these youngsters again."

She nodded slowly, as if she'd already realized it. "They'll go with their uncle and that will be that."

Gabe didn't see any point in mentioning that no one had been able to locate Carlotta's son. Why give Leah something else to worry about, especially if knowing they had a family member who'd step in was a comfort to her?

She squared her shoulders. "Regardless, you need me and I'm not leaving until I absolutely have to."

"Leah..." he warned.

"Please, Gabe? Let me help you, and let me enjoy the extra time with them."

He hated to hear her beg, even though he knew she was only going to put herself through more anguish.

"Yes," she added as if she'd read his thoughts, "I'll probably get teary-eyed and cry most of the way home, but I'm preparing myself for that. I'll be okay. Truly."

Her assurances were convincing, but he knew the separation, when it came, would be far more difficult than she imagined. And yet, if she understood and accepted the risks, what could he do?

"If you're certain..." He was repeating himself again.

"I am."

He hesitated, still unsettled by her choice. "You know I can just toss you on that plane," he mentioned offhandedly. "As the team's leader, I'm responsible for everyone's safety and well-being, including their emotional health."

"You are," she admitted, "but this is my decision, Gabe. I *want* to stay." Her grin widened. "And if you make me leave at first light, I'll return when Sheldon does."

He chuckled as he hugged her tight. "This is against my better judgment, but okay. You can stay."

"Gee, thanks for permission."

He grinned at her wry tone then he added a teasing note to his own to hide his own trepidation. "Are those the only reasons why you don't want to leave—because of the kids and the patients?" He held his breath, hoping to hear she'd had a change of heart about their divorce.

"Oh, I don't know," she said airily. "It could be because you're starting to grow on me, too, but I haven't made up my mind yet."

"And when do you think you might know?" he returned.

"Maybe tomorrow. Maybe next week. Maybe—"

"Right now?" He bent down to brush his lips against hers, but his light kiss soon turned heated. Perhaps it was due to the moonlight or the heady fragrance in the air. Perhaps it was because he was glad Leah wasn't leaving or that this could be their last uninterrupted night for the foreseeable future. Perhaps it was simply because Leah was the one woman who could make his blood sing, but, whatever the reason, he wanted more and he sensed she might feel the same.

"Yes," she breathed. "Maybe now…"

He hauled her against him, eager to take what she was offering and relieved that the moment he'd been waiting for was finally upon him.

"Dr. Gabriel! Dr. Gabriel?"

Leah broke off their kiss. "You're being paged."

Gabe grimaced. "So I hear."

"Maybe it's something minor."

The hopeful note in her voice and the way she'd responded in his arms made him believe that she might be coming round. That she just might have started to look forward instead of backward. That she either had or was on the brink of wanting her future to include him. Those notions were enough for him to accept this most inopportune interruption with grace, even though he really wanted to grumble and complain.

"Are you willing to wager on that?" he asked.

She grinned. "No, but it's a nice thought."

A teenage boy burst into the clearing. "Dr. Gabriel. Dr. Ben says to come."

"Sorry to cancel on you," he told her. "Duty calls."

"I understand. I'm a doctor's wife, remember?"

Leah stretched on the too-thin mattress, noticing Gabe's side was still empty. She'd waited for him to return to their room, but had given up and gone to bed two hours ago. Now her watch dial showed it was nearly midnight and the sheets were cold, which meant the emergency requiring his attention was serious.

She curled around her pillow, feeling like a contented cat as she reflected on their evening. It had felt good to work with Gabe on a professional basis, with none of their old baggage between them. Seeing him in action was a vivid reminder of why she'd fallen in love with him ten years ago. His concern and tireless interest in the people he'd come to serve were glowing testimonies to his character. He was a man who'd move mountains if he could for the people he cared about.

He'd told her that he'd pressed for the adoption for *her*, but she'd never quite believed that, until now. After seeing him in action—seeing how quickly he responded to whatever need he found—she finally believed his motives. And, for the first time, she began to wonder if she might be wrong about other things. Maybe they *wouldn't* be better off being apart…

Although the joy on Gabe's face as he played with Carlotta's grandchildren lay heavily on her chest. Could she open herself up to the possible heartbreak if she agreed to reopen their adoption case file? And were they strong enough as a couple to weather another rejection? Was Gabe that sure that they would be okay so long as they were together? Was she?

These questions went unanswered as their bedroom door swung open and the light from the hallway spilled inside.

"You're awake," Gabe said.

"Barely." She stifled a yawn. "What's going on?"

He tugged on the blanket. "I need a scrub nurse and you're it."

"A scrub nurse? I haven't been in the operating room since I was in training."

"Which still makes you more qualified than the other nurses." He tossed a pair of jeans and a shirt at her. "Come on, sleepyhead."

Leah rolled out of bed and stepped into her jeans. "What sort of surgery?"

"Appendectomy."

"Someone we know?"

"No. Five-year-old boy with excruciating belly pain. His symptoms began two days ago and gradually got worse. I've monitored him for the last few hours because his symptoms weren't classic for appendicitis, but his temp has spiked. I don't want to wait."

"Do you think the appendix ruptured?"

"Let's hope not. Here are your shoes."

She slipped on the loafers then followed him through

the silent building as she finger-combed her hair. "Are they equipped to handle surgeries at the clinic?"

"Not really, but we'll make do. I've operated under worse conditions."

"What about instruments?" Her stomach flopped like a landed fish. "Don't tell me you're going to cut on someone with only a pocket knife and a sewing kit in hand."

"I won't. Luckily, I don't leave home without my own basic tools of the trade," he said with a grin. "I've learned that I never know when they'll come in handy. One of the nurses is sterilizing them now."

What a relief! "How's Mrs. Ortiz doing?"

"Not well," he said grimly. "In fact, Ben and Sheldon would have flown her to Mexico City an hour ago, but I need Ben to handle anesthesia. In any case, they're leaving just as soon as I'm finished."

"The baby?" she asked.

"The midwife thinks the baby's showing a few signs of distress. The obstetrician Ben called said Mrs. Ortiz needs a C-section to relieve the pressure on her diaphragm, but I'm hesitant to do it because we can't take care of a preemie. The sooner we can get her to a place equipped for her problems, the better."

Fortunately, the night-shift clinic nurse had followed Gabe's instructions to the letter. His instruments were sterile and the patient was ready. Leah scrubbed beside Gabe, intent on his last-minute instructions and refresher course. Finally, between the drugs Gabe carried as part of his emergency surgical kit and what they found locked in Hector's cabinet, they were ready and their patient was unconscious.

"If we were at home, we could do this laparoscopically," he said offhandedly. "We have to do this the old-fashioned way."

"He won't care," Leah advised. "Now he'll have a scar to brag about."

Gabe's gaze met Leah's. Although she knew he couldn't see it through the mask, she offered a tremulous smile and hoped she wouldn't make a mistake because of her inexperience. As if he'd read her mind, he said, "Take a deep breath. You'll do fine." His eyes twinkled. "I won't be grading you, either."

She chuckled. "Thanks."

"Okay, then." He flexed his shoulders then held out his hand. "Scalpel."

As soon as she slapped the requested instrument into his hand, she was amazed at how quickly she fell into a rhythm. It was mainly due to Gabe, she had no doubt. His skill was obvious as he cut through skin and tissue until, finally, the offending appendix was revealed.

It was swollen and red and ready to burst.

"Looks like we got here in the nick of time," Gabe said as he clamped, snipped, then eventually sutured. "How's he doing, Ben?"

"Great," Ben said from his place near the patient's head as he monitored vital signs. "Just the way I like surgery—in, out and no problems."

"You can say that again."

After closing his incision and bandaging the site, Gabe pronounced his work done and stripped off his gloves. Looking tired, but pleased, he said, "Let's settle him in his cot, then we'll load Mrs. Ortiz in David's truck. Are you guys ready to go?"

"Corey's at the plane, doing his pre-flight checks," Ben answered. "Sheldon's waiting outside to help us with our patient. Then it's wheels up."

Leah shouldn't have been amazed at their efficiency, but she was. If she didn't know better, she'd think Gabe's team had drilled on this exact scenario until they'd choreographed every step. This was Sheldon's first time in the field and Ben's third, but their united purpose, coupled with Gabe's experience, had pulled them into a well-functioning team.

This was what Gabe had wanted to achieve with this trip—to extrapolate the unity created by this unlikely group of individuals into their marriage—to basically give their relationship a sense of purpose.

Having a family had been part of that purpose and when that had failed, it had seemed pointless to continue the marriage. And yet before Andrew had even become a glimmer in his father's eye, her wish had been simple—to love Gabe and share their lives together. Had that most fundamental purpose changed?

It hadn't, she decided. She still loved him and wanted her life intertwined with his.

Blurting out her revelation was tempting, but it would have to wait. Not only did they have a patient to oversee, but after everything they'd gone through, they both needed to mark the occasion in a special way.

The trip to the airstrip proceeded at a tortoise's pace in deference to Mrs. Ortiz's condition, but eventually everyone and everything had been loaded. The sun was dawning as the plane took off.

Leah watched the aircraft disappear into the cloudless sky. "Strangely enough, I feel like we've been deserted."

Gabe flung an arm around her shoulders. "It does, but at least we have each other." He kissed her forehead. "So, my dear, shall we see if there's any breakfast left?"

Before she could answer, a boy about twelve years old burst into the clearing. "Dr. Gabriel," he called out, panting.

Leah paused, watching Gabe as he listened to the boy's rapid-fire Spanish. She caught a few words, *orphanage* and *hospital*, and guessed at the rest. Finally, he faced her and motioned to the truck. "The sun is barely up and we're already in high demand."

"I gathered as much."

"You're needed at the orphanage and Hector insists on seeing patients even though he can barely stand. I think breakfast is on hold."

"I'm going to predict we'll be busy today."

"So busy you may wish you'd left with the others," he said darkly.

Leah gazed at her husband's face, noticing the distinct shadow of whiskers on his jaw. They would be pushed to their limits, especially Gabe, but she would be there to watch over him and ease his burden as much as possible.

"Not a chance," she said. "I'm exactly where I belong. With you."

CHAPTER ELEVEN

WHEN Leah arrived at the orphanage a short time later, she discovered five more children were symptomatic, bringing her total of sick children to seven. After tending each one personally, it was nearly lunchtime. Anna grabbed her hand and led her to their table, so in between wolfing down her own meal she helped feed the crowd of little people by encouraging them to eat, filling cups, and wiping up the inevitable spills.

As she finished scrubbing the last face before sending them outside to play, one of David's assistants approached her, looking harried. That seemed to be a common trait among everyone she'd seen the past few days. No doubt she would look the same by the end of the week.

"Carlotta is asking for you," the young woman said. "She is in her room."

"I'll be right there."

"Oh, and she wants you to bring…" She mimicked holding something between her thumb and forefinger and made sweeping motions with her hand.

"Pencil and paper?" Leah guessed, wishing she had a better command of the language than she did.

"*Sí*. Pencil and paper."

"I'll bring them," she promised, before washing her hands thoroughly. If only she'd asked Sheldon to include a few gallons of waterless bacterial cleanser… Her skin was already chapped from the constant handwashing and harsh soap, but better to have rough hands than flu.

Inside Carlotta's room and armed with the requested paper and pencil, she was amazed at how quickly the older woman's condition had deteriorated. "Carlotta?" she whispered, lightly touching the woman's shoulder. "You wanted to see me?"

Immediately the woman opened her eyes and struggled to smile. "*Sí.*"

"How are you feeling?" Leah asked. "Do you need any pain pills or—?"

Carlotta waved aside her question. "No. Tell me, Leah, what do you think of my little ones? Do you have what you call a soft spot for them?"

"I do," she admitted, smiling. "They are special children, but you know that better than I."

The older woman's face held that soft, far-off expression, as if she were seeing into the past. "Their parents were special people, too."

"I'm sure they were."

"I want to tell you about them," she said.

Surprised by the request, and also curious, Leah nodded. "I'd love to hear your story."

"Write it down, please. So you do not forget."

Now she understood Carlotta's request, although why the woman would dictate her personal memories in English instead of in her native Spanish was a mystery. Rather than argue with the frail woman, she simply nodded and prepared to write.

"My son, Mario, was a beautiful baby and looked much as José does now," Carlotta began. "We knew his wife's family well, long before he and Jacinta took their vows. She was such a happy child and loved to sing and dance. Anna takes after her. Rosa…my Rosa is, what do you call it…?" She paused to think. "A mixture of both."

"And because of that, all three are a comfort to you."

"Ah, *sí.* That they are. Mario was such a busy boy and as a youth, he…"

For the next hour, Leah recorded everything Carlotta shared. By the time she'd finished her fifth page, Carlotta's voice had faded. "We will continue tomorrow," she said faintly.

"Of course." Leah rose. "Rest now." Before she could move away from the bed, Carlotta grabbed Leah's arm in a surprisingly fierce grip.

"You will watch over my little ones?"

Leah didn't have the heart to explain her stay in Ciuflores wouldn't last longer than a week, and with their uncle presumably on his way it wouldn't be necessary for long. However, she also understood the dying woman's concern, so she folded Carlotta's hand in hers. "Of course. We all will."

Carlotta closed her eyes and nodded. "Come tomorrow."

Suspecting she would continue her story, Leah nodded. "I'll be here."

"Padre."

She paused. "Do you want Father David?"

At Carlotta's weak nod, Leah said, "I'll send him to you."

Rosa was waiting for her outside Carlotta's room, so Leah hoisted her on one hip as she searched out the priest. Fortunately, she found him in the chapel, on his knees. She would have tiptoed away to leave him to his prayers but Rosa began babbling and caught his attention.

"I'm sorry to interrupt," she told him as he approached. "But I spent the last hour with Carlotta. She wants to see you."

"Okay, I'll drop by for a visit. How is she?"

"Weak."

David nodded, his concern obvious in his eyes.

Leah blew a raspberry against the little girl's neck, causing her to giggle. "Would you mind taking her?" she asked, passing Rosa to him. "I want to check on the boy who had surgery and Rosa doesn't belong in the hospital."

"Ah, yes. I heard about Tomas. How is he?"

"His surgery went well and now I want to monitor his post-op care. Not that your nurses aren't doing a good job," she hastened to explain, "but…"

He grinned. "But you want to see for yourself."

Leah felt her face warm. "Yeah."

"I'll tell you what I told Gabe. Don't bite off more than you can chew. We can't afford for you and Gabe to follow in Hector's footsteps."

"I'll be careful," she promised.

Three days later, she finally admitted she had failed to keep her promise. She had tried to follow David's advice—she really had—but there was so much to do and so little time. Between sick children at the orphanage, helping at the clinic, and playing with Carlotta's grandchildren, her days didn't end until she fell into bed each night and curled around Gabe for a few hours before the routine repeated itself.

Today, though, she had the added job of using her ER skills while Gabe tended a man with severe burns on his arms and face.

"Will you keep him here?" she asked Gabe after they left the fellow to rest.

"He'll need skin grafts and surgical debridement, which is beyond what we can provide. According to Hector, there's a town about a half a day's drive away which is the equivalent of our county seat. They have a small hospital that's better equipped than our clinic. One of his friends will deliver our patient and his wife there as soon as she packs a bag."

"One thing you have to admit," she mused aloud, "everyone in this community pulls together. They don't have much, but what they do have, they're willing to share."

"You'll find that attitude in a lot of places like this."

She thought of something else he'd said. "You'd mentioned Hector. Is he feeling better?"

"Yeah, but he's still weak. I told him to concentrate on regaining his strength because when we leave, he'll need to run at peak efficiency." He rubbed his whisker-darkened face, which obviously hadn't felt a razor yet today and it was already mid-afternoon. "I don't envy him at all."

At first glance, her husband looked as perky as he always

did, but she saw the tired set to his mouth and the faint smudges under his eyes. No doubt she probably looked worse.

"Why don't you take a power nap?" she suggested. "Thirty minutes and you'll feel like a new man."

"As tempting as it sounds, I'll have to take a rain check."

"Okay." She stood on tiptoe to deliver a kiss. "I'll see you at dinner in about an hour."

His face lit with curiosity, then satisfaction. "Count on it," he said.

She'd just walked through the door and into what passed as a street when a teenage girl ran up to her. "Señora Gabriel," she panted. "Come!"

Life in Ciuflores seemed to be one crisis after another. "What's wrong?"

"The midwife…she is sick and my sister needs her. We must hurry."

Surely she wasn't asking Leah to deliver a baby! She turned toward the hospital. "I'll get Dr. Ga—"

The girl tugged on her arm. "No time. We must go *now*."

After casting a longing look at the building where her husband was probably dealing with his own crisis, Leah decided to accompany the girl and assess the situation.

The bungalow at the south end of the village was like so many others in its need for repairs and paint, but inside she soon realized she was caught in the middle of a situation she'd always hoped to avoid…the young mother, a girl of about eighteen, was fully dilated and moaning in pain, while her young husband appeared as if he wanted to join in.

Sensing the man would handle a task better than he seemed to handle his laboring wife, Leah sent him to the clinic with a message for Gabe.

Obviously grateful and eager for something to do, he ran out of the house while Leah turned to the younger sister. "Do you have hot water and blankets, um, what's your name?"

"Isabella. My sister is Regina."

"Okay, Isabella. Do you have the things I asked for?"

The girl bobbed her head. "*Sí*. They are ready from the last time."

"The last time?" Leah echoed. It was comforting to know that Regina had gone through this before and wouldn't be a stranger to what was about to happen. "She has another baby?"

"No. It was born dead."

Oh, dear. No wonder both parents looked as if they were frightened out of their wits. The thought of being responsible for bringing their baby into the world with a history like that only added to Leah's pressure.

She couldn't cave in, though. She had to do this. While she wasn't a midwife, her skills were better than nothing until Gabe arrived.

Unfortunately, while Leah washed her hands and changed the sheets with Isabella's help, Regina's contractions began to run into each other without stopping. Another look showed the baby's head was crowning and there was nothing she could do to stop it. She only hoped there wouldn't be any complications before Gabe galloped to the rescue.

She glanced at the door, willing him to suddenly save the day, but he didn't. She was on her own.

"Okay, Regina," she soothed as she positioned herself between the woman's legs. "We're going to do this. You'll be fine and so will your baby. Are you hoping for a boy or a girl? I'm sure you don't care, as long as it's healthy," she chattered on, mainly to draw Regina's attention away from her pain. Although Leah had no idea if the young mother understood her or not, her soothing tone seemed to calm the stark fear in Regina's eyes.

A mighty push later, and the baby's head was free. While Leah suctioned out its nose and mouth, Gabe strode in.

"You seem to have everything under control," he commented as he gently nudged Isabella out of the way to stand beside Leah.

"Thank heavens you're here," she said, relieved she didn't have to do this alone. "You can take over."

"You're doing fine as you are," he said, making no move to usurp her place. "I'll look over your shoulder and talk you through the rest."

He spoke to Regina in Spanish and as she bore down again, one tiny shoulder slipped out, then the other, until finally the little body glided into Leah's hands, already wailing.

"Slippery little things, aren't they?" he commented.

"Yeah." It was an awesome moment, but she didn't have time to revel in it. "You can tell her she has a daughter."

The new mother leaned against the pillow, perspiring and obviously spent as she rattled on and on in Spanish.

Gabe answered calmly as he helped Leah cut the cord. "I told her the baby is fine," he said. "She was worried."

"Rightfully so. She lost her first baby. Stillbirth."

Gabe washed his hands while refreshing her memory on cutting the cord. As soon as she'd finished, and he'd wrapped the baby in the blanket Isabella had provided, he handed her the infant.

"Score her Apgar and let Mom and Dad meet their daughter. I'll finish up. You did great, by the way."

"Regina did all the work," she said. "I basically watched."

After assessing the baby at a ten on the Apgar scale which evaluated her breathing, heart rate, color, muscle tone and response to stimuli, Leah diapered and bundled her up to meet her impatient parents.

Just as she was ready to carry the baby back across the room to Regina, Gabe stopped for a look. "You have the touch," he commented. "She hasn't complained at all about leaving her little nest."

Leah grinned. "Not yet, anyway."

"And look at all that black hair," he commented. "I already see pigtails in her future."

Leah smoothed down the spiky tufts and slid an inexpertly knitted cap over her head. "Between her mom and her aunt…" she smiled at a beaming Isabella "…pigtails, braids and ponytails won't be a problem."

After staying long enough to help Regina freshen up, recite a list of do's and don'ts, and congratulate the new parents, she walked out of the two-room home with Gabe beside her.

"Are you ready to add 'midwife' to your résumé?" he teased.

"Not a chance," she said. "I'm happy with heart attacks, gunshot wounds and stabbings. Those aren't nearly as stressful. The entire time my hands were shaking and my knees wobbled."

"You didn't show it," he said.

"You weren't looking hard enough to see the signs," she responded. "All I could think about was what if this baby didn't survive, either? I didn't want them to blame me for doing something wrong."

Gabe couldn't have asked for a better opening. "Did you blame me when you lost Andrew?"

She froze in her tracks. "Blame you? Why?"

"Because I wasn't there when you started hemorrhaging."

"No." She began walking again. "You hadn't gone on a trip for months and my obstetrician said everything was fine. If she didn't anticipate a problem, why should you? Besides…" she grinned, as if remembering "…by then you were driving me crazy with all of your hovering and I didn't see why you shouldn't go."

He saw her smile fade. "The question is," she asked, "do you blame *me*?"

He frowned. "Why should I?"

"Because, ultimately, I'm responsible for what happened," she whispered, staring straight ahead as if unable to meet his gaze.

"You just said your doctor believed everything was fine. Why do you think you were at fault?"

She shrugged. "Logically, I know what everyone told me, but I can't help wondering if I'd done too much that morning. I'd wanted to prove to you that I might be pregnant but I wasn't helpless. Maybe crawling on the ladder to change a light bulb tore something loose when I reached for the fixture—"

He hated hearing her sound so defeated. He grabbed her arm and pulled her to a halt. "Stop that," he scolded. "It wasn't your fault. It could have happened if you'd been lying on the sofa all day."

Her eyes shimmered. "I know that in my head, but in here…" she tapped her chest "…it's still hard to accept. Especially when you acted as if you couldn't bear to be around me. Which was why I thought you blamed me…"

"I felt helpless because I didn't know how to break through your misery, but I never considered you at fault," he insisted. "What happened was a tragedy, but a divorce wasn't the solution."

"Maybe not, but it would have allowed you to have the things you always wanted."

"I have what I want, right here."

"That's sweet of you to say, Gabe." She began walking and he matched his pace to hers.

"It's true, not sweet," he corrected.

She fell silent, as if sorting things through in her mind, and he didn't interrupt.

"Do you think about them, Gabe?" she finally asked.

He hadn't expected that question. "Nearly every day. Especially when I see children about the same ages as they would be now."

"Really?" she sounded surprised. "You never mentioned a word or acted as if you gave them another thought."

"You weren't looking hard enough to see the signs." He repeated her earlier comment, hoping it would jar her memory.

"I suppose not," she answered ruefully.

"What about you? Do you think about them?"

"I do," she said as she tucked her hands back into her pockets. "I told myself I shouldn't, but different things would happen or be said and I'd be reminded, especially if I heard of another Andrew or an Elizabeth."

"You were going to call her Lizzie."

"Yeah," she said with a far-away expression on her face. "Of all the things we chose I had the most fun deciding on names. A name is so important to a child's self-image."

"It is," he agreed. "Andrew John and Elizabeth Anne, with an 'e'. 'A special spelling for a special baby', you said."

For a long moment they walked in silence, but it wasn't uncomfortable or oppressive. In fact, it seemed almost contemplative, as if it was finally okay to mention those names aloud.

"I didn't want the divorce because I hated you," she said without preamble. "Ending our marriage seemed like the best solution to a bad situation. You'd asked me before if I was trying to save you and, yes, I was. You'd done the same thing for me so many times and this was something I could do for you. I wanted you to be happy because subconsciously I loved you. How else could this trip have opened my eyes so quickly, unless the truth had been there all along, waiting for me to see it?"

"And now?" A combination of anticipation and dread made him unable to breathe.

"I still love you," she repeated. "I want what we had before, even though I have trouble believing it's within reach."

His pulse skipped a beat. "Our future is yours for the taking," he promised. "I'll show you."

"I want it all, Gabe. The love, the passion, the romance, the honesty, the sharing. *Everything.*"

"You'll have it," he said. "And then some."

She stopped on the path leading to the orphanage's front door. "I want our future to begin now, Gabe. Not when we get home, but *now.* I'm tired of feeling empty inside."

He hesitated, not wanting to misinterpret. It would literally destroy him if they made love and she still demanded a divorce. "You said we wouldn't make love because it clouded our issues. Does this mean I can shred those papers in my desk drawer?"

"Yes, you can."

"And our marriage will begin right now," he pressed.

"Unless you're too tired." She raised an eyebrow in question.

His previous exhaustion vanished and he was positively certain he wore a goofy grin on his face. "I'm not too tired."

A tiny wrinkle marred her brow. "I'll bet you haven't eaten all day. Maybe we should—"

"The only thing I'm hungry for is you," he said.

With Gabe having earned her cooperation, he seemed as if he couldn't walk to their room fast enough. He grabbed her hand in an unbreakable grip and pulled her into the orphanage, through the common rooms and to the staff quarters without breaking his stride.

"Gabe," she warned with a smile, "if anyone sees us, they'll wonder if there's a fire."

"They'd be right," he answered with a wink and a smile.

Fortunately they didn't meet a single soul, although there had been two close calls. As soon as they shut the bedroom door, Gabe slid the deadbolt home.

"So we don't have three little interruptions," he said.

In the blink of an eye, buttons were undone, zippers unzipped, and Gabe was following her onto the hastily turned-down bed. Impatient for him, she wriggled underneath his lanky frame.

"We have to slow down." His voice was pained.

She froze. "I'm hurting you. Is it your ribs?"

As she made a move to roll out from under him, he held her firmly in place. "You're not hurting me. I just don't want this to be over too soon," he finished hoarsely.

She studied his lean face, noticing how time had added a few wrinkles around his eyes and a few strands of silver near his temples. In spite of those small changes, he was still the guy who made every other man pale in comparison.

"If it is, then we can look forward to next time."

"I want this to be good for you…" he mumbled in her hair.

"It will be."

As she trailed her hands along his body, the evidence of his previous ordeal seemed to be fading. The ridges, hollows and bumps she'd seen in the hospital weren't as pronounced, but none of that seemed important. Loving her husband was the only thing on her mind.

With the speed of a starving man eating his first meal, he drove her to the brink until she soared over the edge and took him with her.

Too spent to move, she was only vaguely conscious of Gabe drawing the sheet over them before he tucked her under his arm.

"Are you okay?" he asked.

"Oh, yes. You?"

"Never better."

"Your ribs? I didn't hurt you, did I?"

"You didn't and even if you had, the pain would have been worth it. Now, stop worrying about my aches. You're ruining the mood," he teased.

"Can't have that," she answered with a satisfied chuckle. As she rested against him, she saw the sun still shining through white cotton curtains covering the western window. It was far too early to turn in for the night, but she was content to lie in this very spot until morning and savor his touch during every moment. "I can't move," she said, certain he'd turned her into a boneless jellyfish.

"Good, because you're where I want you," he murmured as he nuzzled her temple. "That was…fantastic."

"It was pretty amazing," she agreed.

"What's really amazing is how badly I want you again."

She met his obsidian-eyed gaze. "Really?"

"Oh, really," he said firmly as he rolled slightly toward her so she could discover the truth for herself.

"Mmm," she said, pleased by his response. "Maybe we should pace ourselves."

"Pace ourselves? I don't think I can."

"Try," she ordered, pleased because she was responsible for

his lack-of-control issues. What woman wouldn't be thrilled to know she could drive her man wild?

"What if I don't want to?"

That was better yet. "We have all night," she reminded him.

"True." He kissed her collarbone before nibbling his way south. "But humor me. I'm making up for lost time."

The next morning Leah was certain everyone was wondering where she and Gabe had disappeared to the previous evening. They'd missed dinner and although Gabe had slipped out around nine to check on a patient, he'd returned shortly after and they'd spent the rest of the night enjoying each other, uninterrupted.

Although they hadn't slept very much, Leah felt energized and was pleased to see the spring in Gabe's step as they ambled to the dining hall for breakfast.

The Salazar children immediately descended on them and halfway through their meal, Gabe suddenly announced, "I forgot. David wants to talk to us."

"Oh, Gabe. You don't suppose someone heard us raiding the kitchen before midnight, do you?"

He grinned. "I doubt if he's calling us on the carpet for something so minor. He knows doctors don't always eat on schedule."

"Then I wonder what's on his mind?"

"I don't know, but he'd asked for us to meet him yesterday."

"Yesterday?"

"I got the message right before Regina's husband came barreling into the clinic, yelling for me. After that, for some strange, inexplicable reason..." he grinned "...David's request slipped my mind."

"Ah, so if he's unhappy with us, you'll say it was my fault?" she teased.

"Would you rather I said I was with a patient? For shame,"

he tutted melodramatically. "I can't believe you'd ask me to lie to a priest."

She leaned closer and kissed him, uncaring that Rosa, José and Anna were watching them with unabashed interest. "Whatever. But why do I feel as if we're being summoned to the principal's office?" she joked.

"I don't know. Have you done something wrong?" he returned in the same vein.

"Not that I know of."

Her feeling rose to full strength as David welcomed them into his private office thirty minutes later. He motioned them to take a seat before he perched on the edge of his battered desk.

"You two look chipper this morning," the priest said with a knowing gleam in his eyes.

"We finally got a good night's rest," Gabe answered, squeezing Leah's hand.

"I'm glad to hear it." His expression became serious. "Now, more than ever, you need to take care of yourselves."

David's tone raised Leah's suspicions. He'd called them in for a reason. A very important reason.

Gabe must have sensed the same thing because his smile died. "Why now, more than ever?"

"Because I visited with Carlotta yesterday afternoon," David said simply. "She wants to pass guardianship of her grandchildren to you."

CHAPTER TWELVE

GABE didn't have to see the surprise on Leah's face. From her sharp gasp he knew it was there. The problem was, he didn't know how Leah would respond to such a request and he wished he'd cornered David before this meeting. As much as he would be willing to say yes, he didn't want to pressure Leah one way or the other.

"What did you say?" she asked.

"Carlotta would like you two to be her grandchildren's guardians. Adoptive parents, if you will."

"Oh, my," she breathed. "How? Why?"

"As Gabe knows, Carlotta and I have talked about her grandchildren's future from the time she first became ill," David went on. "While growing up in the orphanage is okay because she knows all of the staff, she wants her grandchildren to be placed with a family. However, she doesn't want them split up, which poses somewhat of a problem. Not many people are willing to take on three youngsters under the age of five at once."

"Of course," Leah murmured.

"In any case," he continued, "after meeting you, Leah, and watching the way you interacted with them, she thought you and Gabe were the couple she'd been praying for."

Once again, Gabe exchanged a glance with Leah. "We're honored, but—"

"But is she sure about this?" Leah interrupted, looking as

if she wasn't willing to let herself believe her good fortune. "I mean, she hardly knows us. Or me anyway."

"She apparently saw enough to be satisfied," David replied. "When she asked my opinion, I agreed with her."

"Thanks for the vote of confidence," Gabe said.

"Anyone who is willing to put the needs of so many ahead of his own is a special individual," he said, "whether they're my friend or not. In any case, on the advice of the lawyer who handles orphanage business, Carlotta has signed a document indicating her wishes. She'll transfer guardianship of Rosa, Anna and José to you to become effective on her death, providing you agree to take all three."

Leah gasped then faced Gabe with something akin to fear in her eyes. "Gabe?" she asked tremulously. "As much as I'd like to say yes, I'm not sure."

He reached out and took her hand. "Like I told you before, the decision is yours."

She met his gaze, as if trying to read his thoughts, before her expression turned speculative. "David," she said quietly, "would you mind giving Gabe and me a few minutes of privacy?"

"Sure. I'll be outside when you're finished."

From Leah's expression, Gabe knew he was in for a rough ride. It began as soon as David closed the door behind him and she jumped up to pace.

For a few seconds Leah couldn't find the words to voice her displeasure, but when she did, she delivered them fiercely. "You don't seem very surprised by David's announcement," she accused.

"I am, and yet I'm not. I wondered if this might be coming."

Her eyes narrowed. "You did? How?"

"Remember the day you held Rosa and the other two showed off their toys? Carlotta and I watched you. In her next breath, Carlotta started talking, hinting actually, about how she wanted a couple like us to take her grandchildren."

"And you didn't say anything? Didn't you think this was something I'd be interested in knowing?"

"What could I tell you? Carlotta said she wanted a couple *like us*, she didn't say she wanted *us*, specifically," he defended.

"You're splitting hairs, Gabe. Admit it. You suspected this was coming." An unpleasant idea occurred to her. "Was *this* why you wanted me to come to Ciuflores with you? To manipulate me—?"

"There you go again, giving me motives I don't have and never did," he ground out. "Like I said before, the choice to adopt is yours. All you have to do is say no, and the discussion ends here. David will understand."

She wanted to run away and avoid facing the issue, but the picture of Carlotta as she'd reminisced about her children, then her grandchildren, stopped her. *David might understand, but will Carlotta?* she wondered.

Leah didn't realize she'd spoken her thoughts until Gabe answered. "She's bound to be disappointed. It isn't like she has plenty of time to put her affairs in order."

No, she didn't. When Leah had seen the woman yesterday, she'd been much weaker than the day before.

"I only know one thing," he continued. "As much as I'd love to accept those three, I won't do it at the expense of our marriage. It took us too long to get where we are today."

Immediately, she regretted her accusations. "I'm sorry for being so sensitive and jumping to the wrong conclusions," she said in a small voice. "I know you better than that. Will you forgive me?"

"You're my wife," he said simply. "We're going to make a mistake here and there." He paused. "Shall we call David back in?"

Don't let fear influence your decision.

"Please do."

Although Gabe seemed curious about her answer, he didn't press her. Instead, he simply squared his shoulders as if bracing himself for bad news.

As soon as David returned, Leah didn't delay in putting both men out of their proverbial misery. She met Gabe's gaze as she announced, "We accept Carlotta's offer."

"Don't do this for me, Leah," Gabe warned.

"I'm not. I'm doing it for *me*, and for *us*."

His smile immediately grew from ear to ear and the tension in his shoulders eased visibly.

"Taking on three is a big responsibility, even without the culture and language issues," David warned. "This will be a major adjustment for all of you."

"We'll handle it," Gabe assured him.

"Definitely," Leah added.

David rose. "I know you will," he said kindly, "but I had to ask. I'm happy for you both and I'm happy for the peace of mind you're giving Carlotta."

"I do have one question, though," Leah said. "What about Carlotta's son—the children's uncle?"

"No one has seen or heard from him in five years. Even if we found him, a judge should honor Carlotta's wishes. I'm not expecting any problems."

Relieved to hear that, she and Gabe headed for the door. "We'd like to thank her for her gift. No, *three* gifts."

David showed them to the door. "She'd like that. Even though I've assured her you'll accept, hearing it for herself will ease her worries. This situation, as sad as it is for her, is also a blessing in disguise for you. So, congratulations."

"Thanks." Gabe shook his hand. "Whatever you need, just say the word and it'll be yours."

David chuckled. "I'll keep your promise in mind. Run along, now, so I can take care of the paperwork to satisfy the legal eagles."

In the hallway, Leah suddenly stopped short. "Oh, Gabe," she wailed as she truly realized what they'd done. "Have we done the right thing? One child is a challenge and two is even more so. But *three*?"

"And here we thought we'd go home to a quiet existence," he joked. "Those days are definitely over."

Leah grinned, already picturing noisy days ahead. "Oh, but just think. Rosa, Anna and José will be *ours*." Her smile dimmed. "I only wish they wouldn't have to lose their grandmother for it to happen, though. I want to celebrate, but a celebration doesn't quite seem appropriate."

"I know, honey." He drew her close. "I think she'd like us to be happy about her decision, especially because her outcome will be the same whether we agree to her offer or not. At least this way she has peace about the future of her grandchildren and we're blessed with the family we've always wanted."

As Leah rested her head on his shoulder, one word reverberated through her mind. *Family.* She and Gabe would be more than a couple, they would be a family. They'd experience all the joys and trials that came with that. She only hoped she'd be worthy of the task.

Suddenly she pulled away. "Oh, my gosh. We have so much to do to get ready for them. Our house will be stuffed to the rafters."

"You always said the place was too big," he teased. "Now you're saying it's too small?"

Love shone out of her eyes. "No, our home is going to be just right."

"How is she?" Leah asked Gabe as he came out of Carlotta's room later that evening.

Gabe tugged her out of the children's earshot. "She's slipped into a coma."

She hated to hear that. She still had so many questions and knew the woman hadn't finished telling her stories. Leah hoped Carlotta had shared her most treasured memories and she took comfort in the notes she'd recorded. Those were definitely precious pages.

"How long?"

"It's hard to say. Could be hours, or days. Not more than that, I would think."

"I'm glad we were able to talk to her for a few minutes this afternoon." A lump formed in Leah's throat as she thought about the emotional scene when she and Gabe had whispered their thanks to the dying woman. Carlotta hadn't answered; she'd simply smiled and wiggled her fingers in their hands.

"I am, too."

"I don't want her to die, but I know she's suffering," Leah admitted. "And I feel selfish for wanting to take the children with us when we leave in a few days. I'd like to stay, and yet I know we can't."

"I wish we could," he said, "but we'll have to leave as soon as they unload the plane."

She didn't like the idea very much and told him so.

"Our mission goes on, Leah," he reminded her. "A long goodbye won't be possible."

"But—" She thought of disappearing from the children's lives without warning or explanation, but Anna was the only one old enough to understand, and even then, she wouldn't. As much as she hated what her attitude said about her, she hoped she could take the children when she left.

"What if Miguel isn't back?" she asked.

"We'll cross that bridge when we come to it." His grim tone suggested he'd already considered the possibility and wasn't looking forward to making the decision.

"On the bright side, the number of new cases seems to be dropping," she offered.

"Let's hope it stays on the downhill slope."

Leah agreed. While over half of the children in the orphanage had exhibited symptoms in the last two days, none of the cases were severe enough to require hospitalization. She and the staff had been able to push enough oral fluids to keep them from becoming dehydrated and with antibiotics readily available for those who'd developed bacterial complications, a lot of problems had been nipped in the bud. So far, Rosa, Anna and José—*her* three children, as she now thought of them—only had a minor case of sniffles.

He flexed his shoulders then threaded his arm around her waist.

"It's getting late, Mrs. Montgomery," he said with the

heated look in his eyes she recognized. "Shall we put our hooligans to bed?"

"Yeah, but after that, what will we do for the rest of the evening?" she asked innocently.

"Don't worry," he answered with a boyish charm. "I'll think of something."

Carlotta slipped away in the predawn hours two days later. Leah could only mourn the loss and marvel in the woman's foresight at requesting Leah write down her family history. At least the three Salazar children would know a little about their roots.

Twenty-four hours after that, Hector had improved to the point where he was working again, although Gabe refused to let him take up his duties for more than a few hours at a time. However, Hector's recovery came as a relief to everyone because their plane was due and Miguel still hadn't returned. Hector might not be functioning at one hundred percent, but if he limited himself to the seriously ill patients, he could manage.

Oddly enough, she'd hated to leave but with these new developments she was impatient for the MMF plane to arrive. First, though, she had to wait for David to return from court with the children's signed and sealed paperwork.

"Would you quit watching the road?" Gabe teased. "David will get back as soon as he can. He won't make you wait a minute longer than necessary."

She bounced José on one hip. "I know. I'm being silly, but we're so close to having everything official. You don't suppose the judge will go against Carlotta's wishes, do you? I mean, David's not an attorney and the document isn't typed up nice and neat."

"I don't know how the Mexican court system works in family cases," Gabe said honestly, "but if anyone can maneuver his way through the system, it's David. Let's not worry until he gets back, shall we?"

Unfortunately, that was the problem. Leah was ready to

make plans and until she could do so with the Mexican government's blessing, she would fret.

When the unmistakable roar of the twin-engined Cessna sounded overhead, Leah's heart sank. She'd privately hoped the plane would be a day or two, or even three, late, but it obviously wasn't meant to be.

By the time they'd greeted Sheldon, unloaded the plane and restocked Hector's supply room, Leah saw David's truck parked near the orphanage. "Oh, Gabe," she breathed. "He's back. I can't wait to hear what he has to say, can you?"

Unfortunately, David's expression was grim, and she didn't like his report.

"The judge went on his circuit this week," David announced.

"Which means?" she demanded.

"He wasn't there to rule on the transfer of guardianship."

"Then when—?"

"The clerk in his office said it will take him at least a month to review the case."

"A month?" She swallowed hard. She'd wanted so badly to take the children home with her now.

"Four weeks won't be so bad, will it?" Gabe asked. "The delay will give us plenty of time to get ready."

"Four weeks is forever to a child," she pointed out. "A veritable lifetime. They won't remember..." Her voice died.

"Yes, they will," Gabe assured her. "They remembered me and they hadn't seen me for several months. A few weeks will pass quickly. This is only a minor inconvenience."

She didn't agree, but arguing with Gabe and David wouldn't change the facts. They couldn't stay and the children couldn't leave. She had to deal with it.

"You're right. We'll need every day of that to get ready," she said, determined to be positive when she felt the opposite.

Gabe hugged her. "That's my girl," he said softly.

David's face remained grave. "Unfortunately, there's more."

Leah's heart sank as she watched Gabe's eyes narrow. "More what?" he asked.

"Carlotta's son Jorge is here." David paused. "He wants the children."

"But—but he can't have them," Leah protested. "Carlotta wanted us to—"

David held up his hands. "I know that. You know that, and Jorge knows that. He believes his mother wasn't in her right mind when she made her decision, especially since she went into a coma a few hours later."

"Is he suggesting she was coerced?"

"He isn't making that accusation directly, but he believes the children belong with the only family they have left. As he's the one in particular..." David shrugged.

Righteous indignation rose up inside her. "Where has he been all this time?" she demanded. "Can he care for three young children?" Her voice wobbled. "Provide for them. *Love* them?"

"That's for the judge to decide, Leah," David said gently. "I'm not happy with this development, either, but what can I do?"

A horrible thought came to her. "Will he...will he take them away? From Ciuflores?" If he did, she was certain she'd never see the children again.

"I've insisted they remain here at the orphanage until the matter is settled. As far as the children are concerned, he's a stranger and they don't need the upheaval right now." He patted her shoulder awkwardly. "I'll keep a close eye on them. I promise."

Leah bit her lip to keep it from trembling. Thankful for Gabe's steadying arm around her, she nodded. "Thanks."

"Should we talk to this clerk to plead our case?" Gabe asked.

"The only one who needs to hear your side is the judge and he's not available. All you can do—and I know this sounds trite—is to go about your usual business while you're waiting."

Inside, she was screaming, *Been there, done that*, but David's advice was sound, even if she didn't like it. As she glanced at Gabe, she saw the same resignation in his eyes.

She managed a tremulous smile. "Then that's what we'll do. If you two will excuse me, I have a bag to finish packing and a few goodbyes to say."

As soon as she'd disappeared, Gabe spoke to David. "There's more, isn't there?"

David exhaled slowly as he ran his finger around his clerical collar. "Yes, and no. I don't have any new information, but I've got to admit, my friend, that this particular judge isn't one I've dealt with before. Rumor has it that he's a tough cookie when it comes to placing children, especially placing them outside the country."

"Then we don't have a chance?" Gabe asked.

"Oh, there's a chance. You have a lot in your favor. Carlotta's blessing will carry a lot of weight."

"Then what's the problem? The judge should understand that if she wanted her son involved, she would have arranged for it."

"According to our attorney, a lot will hinge on Carlotta's health and state of mind at the time she dictated her wishes. Medical testimony will be crucial. Unfortunately—"

"I was the attending physician," Gabe supplied, recognizing the dilemma he was in.

"If Hector had been treating her at the time she faded," David went on, "his opinion would carry more weight than yours because he doesn't have a vested interest in the outcome. You, on the other hand, do."

"It might look that way, but if Jorge wants to reconnect with family, where has he been all this time?" Gabe demanded, incensed on Carlotta's behalf. Perhaps if good old Jorge had been around, Carlotta wouldn't have worked so hard the last several years. Perhaps she would have sought treatment sooner.

"According to him, he travels a lot." As Gabe opened his mouth to argue, David held up his hands. "I know, I know.

Mail goes both ways, but that's a question he'll have to explain to the judge's satisfaction. Personally, I'm hoping Carlotta's wishes will carry the most weight because she knew her son better than anyone. If Jorge argues that he's not the irresponsible man he once was, then the court's decision could rest on who has the most eloquent lawyer."

He cast a meaningful glance at Gabe. "Unless…"

Gabe understood immediately. "Unless we can prove that Jorge isn't the upstanding citizen he claims to be?"

David grinned. "I've met lots of people in my line of work and I can safely say that clothes don't make the man."

Grasping at the hope David had provided, Gabe asked, "What can I do?"

"Nothing. It's easier for me to snoop around because as the orphanage director, I oversee the home placement study." He smiled. "You'd be surprised what sort of connections I have."

"In high places, I hope?"

"To low ones, too." He rose. "I hope you don't mind if I don't see you off. I need to start making phone calls."

"Let me know if I can do anything to help."

"I will. In the meantime, expect the best but prepare for the worst."

Leah fought the tears as she hugged Anna, Rosa and José. "I'll come back," she promised hoarsely. "Be good while I'm gone. When I see you again, we'll have all sorts of fun. We'll read stories and play games…"

"*Adiós?*" Anna asked, her forehead wrinkled in thought.

"Yes, but not for long," Leah told her. "This is just temporary." She tried to think of the right word to use and came up blank. "It's only temporary," she repeated.

Those three words had become her mantra, but it was cold comfort. She had the feeling that once she left Ciuflores, the tenuous tie between her and the children would be cut.

"*Adiós mi abuelita?*" Anna asked.

"No. Not goodbye like your grandmother. I'll see you

again, soon." Knowing the three had seen plenty of weepy people since their grandmother's death, Leah was determined to put on a bright face. Yet as she wrapped her arms around each little wiggly body and received a sloppy kiss, her breath burned in her chest.

Overcome, she glanced at Eva, one of the orphanage's staff, who immediately spoke to the children in a lilting voice that didn't quite match her red-rimmed eyes. Herding the children in front of her, the girl left the room wearing an apologetic expression, leaving Leah alone.

She sat quietly and tried to regain her composure, but the memory of those precious hugs and their baby-clean scent, as well as the moisture remaining on her cheek from Rosa's open-mouthed smooch, made it impossible.

She couldn't leave them. She just couldn't.

Acting on instinct, she dumped her clothes out of her travel case before heading toward the children's room. She began stuffing their things inside with little regard for neatness.

"Leah?"

Ignoring her husband, she doggedly continued her self-appointed task.

He stepped inside. "What are you doing?"

"What does it look like?" She brushed past him to retrieve the two small picture frames on their dresser—pictures which she knew were of their parents. "I'm packing their things. I'd buy everything new, but having a few familiar pieces—"

"Leah," he said firmly, as she stuffed the frames in the suitcase underneath a pile of clothes for protection. "What are you doing?" he repeated firmly.

"I only need a few more minutes, Gabe, and then we can leave."

"If you're doing what I think you're doing—"

She paused, clutching Rosa's doll to her chest. "I'm taking my children home, Gabe. They're mine. Carlotta passed their guardianship to us. She asked me..." Her voice caught.

Gabe gently tugged the doll out of her arms and pulled her against him. "She asked you what?" he coaxed.

The knot of emotion seemed to grow in her throat and she swallowed hard. "Before I knew what she had planned, she asked if I'd watch over them and I promised I would. I can't do that if they're here and I'm not." She met his gaze defiantly. "I won't break my promise."

"Leah," he said kindly. "I understand about promises, but we can't take them with us. Without the proper *legal* papers, we'd be accused of kidnapping."

The sane part of her brain agreed with him, but her heart didn't want to listen. "We have Carlotta's blessing," she argued. "David has it in writing. Duly witnessed. What more do the authorities need?"

"Okay," he said, sounding quite calm, as if they were discussing a grocery delivery. "Say we do it your way. Do you really want to risk the law showing up on our doorstep to haul them away and send us to jail? Or did you plan to live on the lam?"

She wanted to deny the scenario he'd painted would ever happen, but she couldn't. And yet...

"Oh, Gabe, we're so close," she breathed. "I have this feeling that if they don't come with me now, they never will."

His dark-eyed gaze met hers. "It's because we *are* so close that we can't do this. We can't afford to make an impulsive mistake and screw this up."

Logic once again warred with her emotions. "But—"

"If we do everything by the book, we stand a far better chance with the court than if we do something stupid."

"But—"

"Leah," he urged. "Think about this."

"I have, and—"

"Leah." The pity in his eyes was her undoing.

Suddenly, facing the fact she would soon be leaving the children behind, she collapsed against him and wept until his shirt was wet and wrinkled. Once the pain finally subsided, she realized Gabe's strength and support had never wavered in spite of his own heartfelt anguish.

"I thought what we went through before was terrible," she

said when she could finally speak, "but that was nothing compared to this. It's worse because I've gotten to know these three—their likes, dislikes, the way Rosa sucks her thumb when she's tired, how Anna talks with her hands—"

"How José wrinkles his nose when he smiles," he finished as he continued to rub comforting circles on her back. "You're right. This time is much more difficult."

As she stole a glance at his face, his red-rimmed eyes proved he was as torn up about the change in circumstances as she was.

"The good news is," he continued, "our absence is only temporary."

"Only temporary," she echoed as she pulled away.

He rubbed away the tear tracks on her cheeks. "Better?"

"Not really." She managed a weak smile.

"Come on," he said tenderly. "Let's go home."

CHAPTER THIRTEEN

EXPECT the best but prepare for the worst.

Over the next week, Gabe tried his best to follow David's advice, but he hadn't been able to share the same counsel with Leah. If he suggested there was a chance the court wouldn't decide in their favor, he didn't know how she'd react. During the time they'd been home she'd jumped between chatting about what toy each child would like to fretting if they were eating properly, getting enough hug time and staying healthy.

Sitting on the sidelines, as David had also suggested, was impossible. Although he had plenty of faith in his friend, David wasn't the only man with connections and Gabe didn't hesitate to use them. Discreetly, of course.

But by the beginning of the second week his guilt demanded he pull Leah aside.

"I'm going to Mexico tomorrow," he told her.

Her hands flew to her mouth. "You have news?" she breathed, her eyes lighting up.

"No," he said. "I haven't wanted to tell you this because I didn't want to raise your hopes, but you deserve to know the truth. I promised complete honesty when we got back together and I haven't held up my part of the bargain."

"What are you saying, Gabe? What aren't you telling me?"

He drew a deep breath, glad she was more interested in his news than in his moral lapse. "David is trying to dig up information on Jorge Salazar and so far he's coming up blank. I'm heading down there to see what I can do."

"I'll go with you."

"No. Absolutely not."

"Gabe," she warned. "I have a vested interest, too."

"Yes, but David says the key is to be discreet. There are places I need to go where you'll stick out like a sore thumb. If Jorge tells the judge we're deliberately trying to sabotage him…we can't take that risk."

"Then I'll stay in Ciuflores."

He shook his head. "I'm headed to Mexico City. This is a fly-in and fly-out trip. I can't work in a detour for you. I'm sorry."

She let out a deep sigh. "Okay. I don't like it, but I understand."

"Good."

"Thanks for being honest," she said. "I know it would have been easier on you to keep me in the dark, but I'm glad I know what you're doing. Just keep me posted, okay?" She grinned. "I know how much you hate to fly."

"Count on it."

Although Leah was glad that Gabe had gotten past his overly protective attitude, she almost wished he *had* left her clueless. The very thing he'd worried about—putting her on an emotional roller coaster—came to pass. Over the next two weeks he flew four more times to Mexico and on the conclusion of each trip he simply shook his head.

Her optimism was fading, but she clung to the idea that on one of his fact-finding missions he'd finally have news that would be in their favor.

And yet she watched Gabe push himself harder and harder, as if he was determined to succeed at any cost. At times she felt as if she was losing him because he became so focused on his objective, which was to bring the Salazar children home. She didn't know what to do or say to warn him about the path they seemed to be on, but the words came to her after the foundation's fundraising gala...

"You're leaving again?" Leah stared at her husband as he stripped off his bow-tie and tossed his tuxedo jacket on their bed at two a.m. She still wore her black shimmery ballgown, minus the strappy heels she'd kicked off the minute they'd walked through the door.

"First thing in the morning."

"It *is* morning," she pointed out.

"At eight," he said. "That gives me..."

"Six hours," she supplied. "That's all the notice I get? Six hours?" She couldn't begin to describe the hurt she felt. "How long have you known you were leaving?"

"I planned this trip yesterday."

"You should have told me."

"You were busy with the last-minute plans for the ball," he pointed out. "Honestly, it slipped my mind."

"It may have, but it's no excuse," she insisted. "You have to slow down, Gabe. You can't keep up this pace."

"Don't worry. I'll sleep on the plane."

"This isn't about sleeping, although you *are* burning both ends of the candle," she said tartly.

"I'm doing this for you, Leah. For us."

"I understand." She sank onto the bed and began toying with a loose sequin. "Tonight, when I saw the picture of me and the children on the screen..." Her throat closed and unconsciously she knotted her dress in her fist. She hated getting emotional and had told herself she wouldn't, but here she was, doing the very thing she'd vowed she wouldn't.

"That photo is my favorite," he said as he sat beside her. "I don't know how or when Sheldon snapped it, but I'm grateful. He's going to give you a copy, by the way."

"Thanks," she said. Seeing the image was a bittersweet experience and would be until the Mexican court finally reached a decision. She was at the point where she was willing to propose they grease a few palms, although she could imagine Gabe's horrified reaction to the suggestion. If he'd nipped her kidnapping attempt in the bud, then he certainly wouldn't be open to her attempt at bribery.

She rubbed her forehead, wondering what her ideas said about her character if she was willing to resort to illegal activities. Then again, she was a desperate woman.

Pushing those thoughts away, she added, "The point is, after seeing those pictures, I...I need you, Gabe, here with me. Not jetting miles and miles away."

He caressed her cheek. "Aw honey, I'd like nothing more than to be here, but this trip is important. I feel as if I'm so *close*."

She held his hand to her face. "You said that last time."

"I know, but—"

"You'd tried to protect me from experiencing emotional ups and downs, but now it's my turn. Please, Gabe, don't go. I know you're trying to give me my heart's desire, but maybe it isn't your place to provide it."

"I want to, though."

She snuggled close. "And I love you for trying, but we need to step back and let David handle things." She paused. "He is still investigating, isn't he?"

As Gabe's nod, she smiled. "Then let him do his job."

He stared at her like a dog staring at a new dish. "What if David doesn't succeed? What if we lose our case?"

"I'll be crushed," she admitted, "but I won't be nearly as devastated as I will be if I lose you. So, please. Promise me this is your last trip."

He looked as if he was ready to protest, but instead he simply nodded. "Okay," he said wearily. "You win."

"Good," she said, relieved by his decision. "Would you like me to drive you to the airport?"

"Thanks, but Sheldon is tagging along so he's picking me up. Meet me when my plane lands on Monday evening?"

Greeting him at the airport when he returned had become part of her routine. She'd added it because she needed the reassurance that he'd arrived safely. The main reason, however, was because she missed him terribly and wanted to see him as soon as possible.

"I'll be there with bells on."

Leah puttered around the house after Gabe left, wanting to do something but unable to find anything interesting enough to hold her interest. She baked a cake, but when it didn't rise, she realized she hadn't added all the ingredients. It landed in the trash.

She sewed a couple of loose buttons on Gabe's shirts then discovered she'd stitched the placket closed. She ripped it out and started over.

She took their formal wear to the dry cleaner's and after arriving at the shop across town realized she had forgotten to bring Gabe's tuxedo pants.

Staying at home and reading a book was pointless because she couldn't remember what she'd read from one page to the next.

Unsettled for reasons she couldn't understand, although she attributed the feeling to Gabe's absence, she meandered again into what she'd tentatively decided would be the girls' room.

Idly, she wondered if Gabe had seen the changes she'd made in here. Granted, they'd only been small ones and had only occurred a few days ago, but for her they were a step forward.

As she looked at the space where the crib had once stood, she reflected on all the "what ifs." What if one or both of their previous adoption attempts had been successful? Gabe wouldn't have insisted she join him on his trip to Ciuflores. She wouldn't have met Carlotta or her three grandchildren.

But even before that, what if Gabe hadn't returned from his plane crash? Or what if he had, and they'd divorced?

Those ideas sent a cold shudder down her spine. Of all the people who'd come and gone in her life, Gabe was her anchor. Whether or not the Mexican government allowed her to keep her promise to Carlotta, she would still have Gabe. He was her rock and she couldn't imagine life without him.

Fortunately, Jeff had taken her announcement in his stride. He'd suspected she hadn't gotten over her husband and was glad he'd allowed her the space she'd needed to figure that out for herself.

As for the children, if fate exacted another pound of flesh and stole her dream again, she would grieve, just as Gabe would. The difference was, they'd do it together, not separately. She loved him too much to fall back into those marriage-destroying old habits. She might never raise children, but she had Gabe and she would fight to keep their marriage alive, even if she had to resign her job and donate her time to the Montgomery Foundation in order to see him.

Strangely enough, her decision chased away her gloom. Over the next twenty-four hours nothing spoiled her good mood or her inner peace—not even what Jane had affectionately termed "another shift from hell".

Fortunately, she was able to leave the hospital promptly at six p.m. on Monday. Forty minutes later, she'd been cleared to wait on the tarmac near their plane's hangar, where she polished off the bottle of soda she'd purchased from a vending machine. Finally, the familiar plane with its red and black markings appeared overhead, and a few minutes later taxied to a stop in front of her.

She stood, eager for Gabe to open the door and descend the stairs. He'd been gone less than forty-eight hours and it seemed like forever.

Finally, the door descended, but no one exited.

"What's taking so long?" she muttered impatiently as she stared at the empty opening.

No sooner had she spoken than Gabe appeared. She strode forward, determined to meet him at the bottom of the steps. "Gabe," she called, waving to capture his attention.

His answering smile was broad. Apparently his trip had turned out better than he'd expected because he seemed happier than he had on previous returns.

She watched him step out, but then, before he carefully descended the stairs, he hoisted a small figure onto one hip. Her steps slowed. What in the world…?

Behind him came a larger child wearing a floral print sundress. This one painstakingly took each step as she held onto the railing with one hand and clutched a familiar doll in the other. Sheldon brought up the rear, carrying another child—a boy.

Leah froze in her tracks as the group come forward. Gabe looked positively ecstatic and the children's eyes were filled with wonder as they took in their surroundings.

The crowning moment came when Anna saw her. A huge grin spread across her little brown face and she ran forward, crying *"Mamacita!"*

Mommy. Leah swore her heart skipped a beat, probably several. Could it be?

She crouched down to hug her. "My goodness, you've grown," she told the youngster in a tear-choked voice. "Gabe?" she asked, hardly able to believe the reality of the little girl in her arms.

Her husband's smile stretched from ear to ear. "Hi, honey. We're finally home."

The look of awe and pure joy on Leah's face made everything Gabe had gone through worth the effort. Gifting her with the Hope diamond wouldn't have made her this happy or been this satisfying.

"Gabe?" she said again as she rose, reaching out tentatively to stroke Rosa's hair, as if afraid the children were only an elaborate hallucination.

He bent his head to drop a swift kiss on her startled mouth. "How do you like the presents I brought?" He held out Rosa, who immediately dove into Leah's arms, confident in Leah's quick reflexes and ability to catch her.

"They're fantastic," she told him, "but how was this possible? Are they here for a visit? When do they go back? Where's

David? Did the judge finally hear our case?" Then, "*Why didn't you tell me?*"

He laughed at her rapid-fire questions. "First things first. Let's get these monkeys in the car."

"But we don't have three car seats," she wailed.

"Yes, you do," Sheldon piped up. "As soon as we knew we were bringing them, I called the office. Loretta found three and stuck them in my car."

It took a while to make the transfer, but she and Gabe soon had everyone buckled into the safety seats and they were on their way. Corey would deliver the rest of their things later.

The children were clearly tired and fussy from their experience, so Leah's questions had to wait. All except one.

"Are they ours, Gabe? To keep?" she asked as he drove out of the airport.

Determined to chase away the fear in her eyes, he nodded. "They're ours. No refunds allowed."

She let out a long, deep, heartfelt breath then turned the most brilliant smile on him as moisture glistened in her eyes. "Thank you," she said as she squeezed his elbow before she looked into the back seat for the tenth time in as many minutes.

Leah smiled at the children behind her. Rosa and José were dozing and Anna was fighting to stay awake, but soon the car's motion lulled her to sleep, too.

The nap during the short drive home completely restored their energy. They were more than ready to eat the crackers and sliced apples she hurriedly assembled before rushing off to play with the toys she and Gabe had purchased beforehand, in anticipation.

"We need an emergency grocery-store run," she informed her husband. "I don't have kid-friendly food in the house."

"I'll go," he advised her. "Or, better yet, call Loretta and give her a list."

She didn't think shopping for groceries fell under the duties of an office assistant, but the woman was a grandmother and under the circumstances, would most likely be thrilled to do it.

"Okay, tell me what happened," she demanded when the youngsters were entertaining themselves with both their old and new toys. "And talk fast because we have a thousand and one things to do."

"After we landed in Mexico City, David called to tell me the judge was holding a preliminary hearing. I wanted to be there to state our case and answer his questions, so we immediately flew to Ciuflores. As it turned out, the investigators David hired had turned up some rather damning information about Jorge. Once the evidence was presented to the court—at the eleventh hour, I might add—the judge ruled in our favor. I thought about waiting until we could bring them home together, but David thought the children would have a difficult time with another separation, even a short one. So, here we are."

"Why do I sense there's more to this story than you're telling me? And where did David find the money to hire an investigator? His services couldn't have been cheap."

Gabe shrugged innocently. "I heard he received an anonymous donation to help defray those costs, but it's purely a rumor. Of course, it would also be pure speculation to guess the identity of the man who personally called in a few favors from some of his own contacts."

"I should be upset with you for leaving me out of all the fun, but I'm not." She stood on tiptoe to swiftly kiss him. "I'm glad you're back, Gabe. If I forgot to tell you this, welcome home."

His midnight-black eyes reflected tenderness. "I know things will be crazy for a while, probably years," he tacked on wryly, "and we may feel harried and hassled, but I'll always make time for us."

She wrapped her arms around his chest. "I intend to hold you to your promise."

The sound of raised voices caught Leah's attention. Clearly, José and Anna were having a difference of opinion. "You may want to rethink your stance on work-related travel," she advised. "A trip may be the only time you experience peace and quiet."

"It might," he agreed, "but peace and quiet can't compare to having a family who needs me."

"And we always will."

JANUARY 2011 HARDBACK TITLES

ROMANCE

Hidden Mistress, Public Wife	Emma Darcy
Jordan St Claire: Dark and Dangerous	Carole Mortimer
The Forbidden Innocent	Sharon Kendrick
Bound to the Greek	Kate Hewitt
The Secretary's Scandalous Secret	Cathy Williams
Ruthless Boss, Dream Baby	Susan Stephens
Prince Voronov's Virgin	Lynn Raye Harris
Mistress, Mother...Wife?	Maggie Cox
With This Fling...	Kelly Hunter
Girls' Guide to Flirting with Danger	Kimberly Lang
Wealthy Australian, Secret Son	Margaret Way
A Winter Proposal	Lucy Gordon
His Diamond Bride	Lucy Gordon
Surprise: Outback Proposal	Jennie Adams
Juggling Briefcase & Baby	Jessica Hart
Deserted Island, Dreamy Ex!	Nicola Marsh
Rescued by the Dreamy Doc	Amy Andrews
Navy Officer to Family Man	Emily Forbes

HISTORICAL

Lady Folbroke's Delicious Deception	Christine Merrill
Breaking the Governess's Rules	Michelle Styles
Her Dark and Dangerous Lord	Anne Herries
How To Marry a Rake	Deb Marlowe

MEDICAL™

Sheikh, Children's Doctor...Husband	Meredith Webber
Six-Week Marriage Miracle	Jessica Matthews
St Piran's: Italian Surgeon, Forbidden Bride	Margaret McDonagh
The Baby Who Stole the Doctor's Heart	Dianne Drake

1210 Gen Std LP

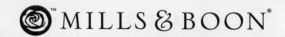

MILLS & BOON®

JANUARY 2011 LARGE PRINT TITLES

ROMANCE

A Stormy Greek Marriage	Lynne Graham
Unworldly Secretary, Untamed Greek	Kim Lawrence
The Sabbides Secret Baby	Jacqueline Baird
The Undoing of de Luca	Kate Hewitt
Cattle Baron Needs a Bride	Margaret Way
Passionate Chef, Ice Queen Boss	Jennie Adams
Sparks Fly with Mr Mayor	Teresa Carpenter
Rescued in a Wedding Dress	Cara Colter

HISTORICAL

Vicar's Daughter to Viscount's Lady	Louise Allen
Chivalrous Rake, Scandalous Lady	Mary Brendan
The Lord's Forced Bride	Anne Herries
Wanted: Mail-Order Mistress	Deborah Hale

MEDICAL™

Dare She Date the Dreamy Doc?	Sarah Morgan
Dr Drop-Dead Gorgeous	Emily Forbes
Her Brooding Italian Surgeon	Fiona Lowe
A Father for Baby Rose	Margaret Barker
Neurosurgeon . . . and Mum!	Kate Hardy
Wedding in Darling Downs	Leah Martyn

FEBRUARY 2011 HARDBACK TITLES

ROMANCE

Flora's Defiance	Lynne Graham
The Reluctant Duke	Carole Mortimer
The Wedding Charade	Melanie Milburne
The Devil Wears Kolovsky	Carol Marinelli
His Unknown Heir	Chantelle Shaw
Princess From the Past	Caitlin Crews
The Inherited Bride	Maisey Yates
Interview with a Playboy	Kathryn Ross
Walk on the Wild Side	Natalie Anderson
Do Not Disturb	Anna Cleary
The Nanny and the CEO	Rebecca Winters
Crown Prince, Pregnant Bride!	Raye Morgan
Friends to Forever	Nikki Logan
Beauty and the Brooding Boss	Barbara Wallace
Three Weddings and a Baby	Fiona Harper
The Last Summer of Being Single	Nina Harrington
Single Dad's Triple Trouble	Fiona Lowe
Midwife, Mother…Italian's Wife	Fiona McArthur

HISTORICAL

Miss in a Man's World	Anne Ashley
Captain Corcoran's Hoyden Bride	Annie Burrows
His Counterfeit Condesa	Joanna Fulford
Rebellious Rake, Innocent Governess	Elizabeth Beacon

MEDICAL™

Cedar Bluff's Most Eligible Bachelor	Laura Iding
Doctor: Diamond in the Rough	Lucy Clark
Becoming Dr Bellini's Bride	Joanna Neil
St Piran's: Daredevil, Doctor…Dad!	Anne Fraser

FEBRUARY 2011 LARGE PRINT TITLES

ROMANCE

The Reluctant Surrender	Penny Jordan
Shameful Secret, Shotgun Wedding	Sharon Kendrick
The Virgin's Choice	Jennie Lucas
Scandal: Unclaimed Love-Child	Melanie Milburne
Accidentally Pregnant!	Rebecca Winters
Star-Crossed Sweethearts	Jackie Braun
A Miracle for His Secret Son	Barbara Hannay
Proud Rancher, Precious Bundle	Donna Alward

HISTORICAL

Lord Portman's Troublesome Wife	Mary Nichols
The Duke's Governess Bride	Miranda Jarrett
Conquered and Seduced	Lyn Randal
The Dark Viscount	Deborah Simmons

MEDICAL™

Wishing for a Miracle	Alison Roberts
The Marry-Me Wish	Alison Roberts
Prince Charming of Harley Street	Anne Fraser
The Heart Doctor and the Baby	Lynne Marshall
The Secret Doctor	Joanna Neil
The Doctor's Double Trouble	Lucy Clark

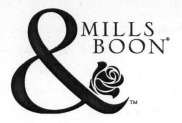